Greenhorn
on the Frontier

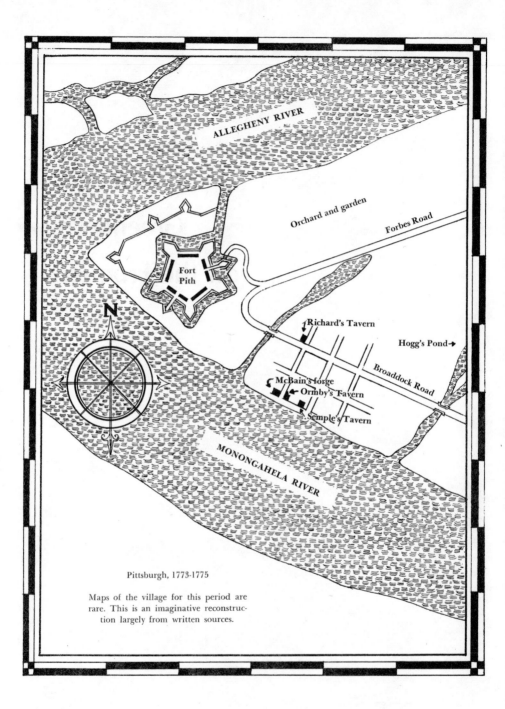

ALLEGHENY RIVER

Orchard and garden

Forbes Road

Fort
Pith

N

Richard's Tavern

Hogg's Pond →

Broaddock Road

McBain's forge

← Ormby's Tavern

Semple's Tavern

MONONGAHELA RIVER

Pittsburgh, 1773-1775

Maps of the village for this period are
rare. This is an imaginative reconstruc-
tion largely from written sources.

Greenhorn on the Frontier

By ANN FINLAYSON

Illustrated by W. T. Mars

FREDERICK WARNE AND COMPANY, INC.   New York & London

For Yah-yah's little girl.

Contents

1.	The Forks	1
2.	Greenhorn	13
3.	Anse	28
4.	A Wedding in Town	40
5.	Their Place	54
6.	Cabin Raising	62
7.	Showanyaw	75
8.	Disputed Territory	85
9.	Maneuvers	98
10.	Alarm	109
11.	Home Defense	121
12.	New Relations	133
13.	Lord Dunmore	144
14.	Possessions	158
15.	Troubles Mount Up	167
16.	Saving Sukey	181
17.	Battle Royal	191
18.	Freedom Papers	206
19.	After Word	209

Greenhorn
on the Frontier

1
The Forks

Harry Warrilow got to his feet and cupped his hands. "Sukey!" he shouted. "I need you!"

His sister had run on ahead, impatient because he had said they were getting close, and she—unlike him—had never seen the town between the rivers.

"Sukey! *Su-ukey!*"

Waiting for a reply, he glanced about him. They *were* getting close, and no mistake. The country was more and more open hereabouts, still hilly but rolling instead of steep, overrun with creeks and seeps and occasional natural meadows in place of the endless forest and beetling rocks. To the south there seemed to be a gap and then more hills. Unless Harry was much mistaken, that was the valley of the Monongahela. Straight ahead, to the west of them, flowed the Allegheny, directly across their path, and their immediate destination was the place where the two great rivers met.

Now if that creek they had passed over this morning
with so much difficulty was Turtle Creek, then there
couldn't be more than a few hills—

But, ah, here came Sukey now, running down the path,
slim ankles flashing. "It's the plaguey cart!" he called to
her angrily. "The broken rim is caught again. If you take
hold of the root, I'll—"

"We're here, Harry!" she cried, her face alight. "It's just
over the rise! Once over the top, it's laid out plain as a
pikestaff."

"What! You mean—?"

"Come *on!*" She reached for his hand.

"But—"

"Oh, bother the silly cart! Leave it! Come see!"

Close, he had thought, but not *that* close. But if she was
right, then this was Grant's Hill, the last obstacle on a long

and difficult road. His own heart began to beat a little faster, his excitement to match Sukey's, as he scrambled up the muddy slopes. On every side, buds were swelling, rust-colored with promise, and the air smelled cold and damp and sweet with spring. They emerged on a broad, almost level hilltop.

"See," said Sukey proudly.

She was right. For no one could stand here, gazing out, and not know he was looking at the Forks of the River Ohio.

They had come a far piece—a hard journey over a rugged road, afoot and pushing the heavy handcart—to stand here. Looking back, Harry was almost awed. They had really done it then—they had crossed the mountains. The first stage of their journey was behind them.

The journey had begun long ago and far away—in England where they were orphaned as children and separated. In Boston, chance had brought them together again, and they had resolved not to waste their good luck. They would be their own masters. They would have a place where they belonged and that belonged to them. They would make a farm and be independent of everyone, and no one could separate them again.

They were poor, though, so that meant settling on the frontier. Well, then, men said the Ohio Valley lands were rich and well watered. Sukey had been all ready to set out immediately, but Harry had held back.

"We have to earn money to buy the land."

"Oh, Harry!" Sukey cried impatiently. "The wilderness is there and waiting. There's plenty of land no one wants. Let's make our farm and worry about getting a deed later."

Harry had shaken his head doggedly. "No, I've heard of too many people who were done out of their hard-won farms by men who come along later with a piece of paper. We'll get our deed first. Besides," he'd added, "I want to be a *good* farmer, and I don't know how yet."

So, they had gone to work for the Wertmüllers on their fat farm in Lancaster County, Pennsylvania, and had earned and saved and learned, and at last the day had come when they were ready to leave—a blustery day in March. The Wertmüllers lined up at the door, kindly and good-natured, to wave good-bye: "Goodt-bye ... Goodt-bye ... *Gottbefohlen* ... Goodt luck ..."

It had not seemed such a difficult journey then or when they boarded Harris's Ferry to cross the Susquehanna. They were buoyed up by the excitement of on-our-way-at-last. Besides, Harry had made the trip once before, to pick out their farm site, so they weren't forging forth into the utterly unknown. Indeed, that day on the ferry, all Harry could think of was how pretty the distant Alleghenies looked.

The first few days it was easy enough. There was only the March wind to fight, whistling down the broad Susquehanna like a cavalry charge, so that Harry had to cover his shoulders with their worn old bearskin and trudge with his head down and insist that Sukey keep to the lee of the cart. Sometimes snow or sleet was added, or the ground froze solid under their moccasins, and they would have to stop, to build a fire and dry out their numb feet. Along about that time, the cartwheel first began to give them trouble, and they had had to trade Sukey's only spare stockings to a blacksmith for a temporary repair. But they did the first fifty miles to Chambersburg in four days.

Then General Forbes's road began to wind upward.

The roadway was only twelve feet wide in most places, hacked from the primitive forests, rutted by the wheels of settlers' wagons and siege guns alike. Some of the stumps still made part of the road bed; in other places it was paved with rock and mud half washed away by the spring freshets. They lost count of the creeks and brooks they crossed on crude log and puncheon bridges, or places where the road had had to be gashed straight from the mountain flanks, leaving scarred patches of raw earth.

Up and up and up again they struggled, Harry pushing the cart, Sukey pulling. They'd had to fashion drag ropes for her, so that she could add her strength to his on the steepest grades. It was his fault that their load was so heavy and that they had come afoot. He had insisted on investing in a pot still. Whiskey would be their cash crop, because whiskey was the easiest way to get grain to market. Sukey had wanted to buy a horse or, barring that, tools.

"Sukey, in the long run, the still is more useful. The still will get us a horse, tools, everything we need."

"We need them now!"

"We'll make do the first year."

"Oh, Harry!" But Harry had learned to give in to her on little things and stick like a rock when something was important to him. He got his still.

So, it shamed him a bit to see her in harness like an animal, and she knew it, and she wasn't the type to reproach him unfairly. The minute the curving road began to level off, to dip a little, she would slip out of the ropes, tuck them under the cart cover, and run ahead to find a place to camp, to light a fire, to stir up johnnycakes for their supper.

At night, they uptilted the cart, and with its cover and

piled-up branches managed to erect some kind of shelter behind which to huddle. Often it snowed. Once they had to spend two days crouched under a lean-to of sticks and bark. They kept a fire going all night, and stretched out their feet to it, Indian fashion, and talked a little before sleeping. There were some good moments, those evenings by their fire.

"Read me the paper, Harry," Sukey would say, hugging her knees.

He was never certain whether she actually enjoyed hearing it read as often as she called for it or just did so because she knew he liked to read it. But he didn't care. He would pull out the painted-cloth cover, open it, remove the big piece of stiff paper, and unfold it with care.

Know all men by these presents that I [and Harry always paused a breath before he spoke that magic name] JOHN PENN, for and in consideration of the summe of twenty-five pounds lawfull money of England to mee in hand paid by Harry Warrilow husbandman and Susannah Warrilow spinster, receipt whereof I do hereby acknowledge, do hereby Give, Grant, and Dispose unto the said Harry Warrilow and the said Susannah Warrilow the full rightt tytle to five hundred Acres of land Situate in a Turn of Olethey Creek in the province of PENSILVANIA, every Acre to be admeasured and computed according to the Dimensions of Acres measured and appointed in and by the Statute made in the three and thirtieth Year of the Reigne of king Edward the first, the said five hundred Acres to be held by the said Harry Warrilow and the said Susannah Warrilow, their heirs and assigns, forever from mee and my heirs and all others in peaceable quietness of possession. In Witness whereof, I have hereunto sett my Hand and Seal. Dated this Eighth Day of December, Anno Domini, 1772.

JOHN PENN
*Governor to their Excellencies
the Lords Proprietaries of the Province
of Pensilvania*

Sukey always did the same thing—sighed, quick and gusty, and said, "Ours. Five hundred acres."

" 'In peaceable quietness of possession,' " Harry liked to repeat. There was reassurance in the term.

Harry always slept better, even with snowflakes blowing into his face, for having read the paper and for knowing it was wrapped up again safe in its case and tied around his waist.

At dawn there was no leisure for reading papers. It was wake up, load the fowling piece, go out and try to bag a squirrel for supper, munch another of those everlasting johnnycakes, and be off.

They passed Fort Loudoun and swung north through a narrow valley to Fort Littleton, then west again across Sideling Hill to Fort Bedford. These had been military posts at one time, but the Regulars had been withdrawn from the frontiers a few months before, and now the forts served as mere trading posts and stopping places for travelers headed west.

Bad as the road was, there were many travelers on it. They encountered Indian traders—rough, smelly men

leading long lines of pelt-laden pack ponies. Rarely one of the great Conestoga wagons would come lurching and jingling by, carrying freight to Pittsburgh at ninepence a pound. There were well-equipped family caravans as well and some few as poor as Harry and Sukey. Now and then a horsebacked man of substance brushed past—an agent of the Penns perhaps—and once they came face to face with a solemn group: blacks manacled together in a long chain, being driven by three white men heavily armed.

Sukey turned white with rage. "Soul drivers!" she cried, glaring after the grim procession. "They'll march them around the countryside until every last one is sold. It's a wicked, wicked evil!"

"All right, Sukey, all right," he said mildly. He had long grown used to Sukey's reaction to slavery.

Up and up and up . . . toiling and trudging and pushing and pulling . . . The blisters on Harry's hands

had long since broken and re-formed and rebroken and begun to make calluses. The ache in his calves from digging his heels into slippery mud slopes had either worn itself out or become so permanent that he no longer noticed, but his back hurt and his shoulders hurt and his forearms hurt and his thighs hurt, and one day as they knelt to drink from an ice-fringed stream, he didn't think he would ever get the strength to stand up again.

"Let's rest a bit, eh?"

"Harry, are you all right?"

He sank to a sitting position and tilted his head back against the cart. "Right as rain in a minute." He moved his aching, creaking limbs to ease their soreness and wished he could loll there forever.

Sukey busied herself fixing some pennyroyal tea, which she made him drink, and just as he was finishing it, a traveler appeared out of the woods, wearing the deerhide leggings and homespun hunting shirt of a backcountry man. They exchanged greetings as he drank from the creek and idly discussed origins and destinations. The stranger nodded at the creek from which he had just drunk. "Western waters now," he said. And lifting a couple of fingers at them, he was off.

"What did he mean, Harry?"

"Why," he said slowly, trying to remember his geography, "this creek—it flows into the Conemaugh, and the Conemaugh into the Kiskeminetas, and the Kisky into the Allegheny." His breath came a little short. "These are westward flowing waters. From here they run clear down to New Spain."

"Then we've crossed! The worst is behind us."

"We've crossed, yes," he said. He would not complete the promise because stony Laurel Hill and Chestnut Ridge still barred their path. But he got to his feet and picked up the cart handles with new strength.

The road wound upward once more, through a region where dense forest alternated with great outcrops of virgin rock, and the stony path was hard on their soft-shod feet. At night they heard cougars scream, and they were told that wolves roamed the forests. But now all the signs were of spring. Mud mired their feet, and the great tangled thickets of grapevine and creeper, which draped trees, bushes, rocks, everything with a perfect blanket of growth, showed fat leaf buds and fresh new reaching tendrils.

From time to time they came to what was called a tavern, though these were little more than cabins offering a corner of the garret to sleep in. The only refreshment was whatever the family could spare. The Warrilows rarely stopped at one. They had little extra money and were saving it for a treat when they should reach Pittsburgh.

They passed Fort Ligonier, the last of the stockades along the Forbes, and then there was only Chestnut Hill, the westernmost ridge. Then somehow that, too, was surmounted, and there was nothing left but Hannastown and the rolling hills and Turtle Creek, and now even those were behind them, and they stood on Grant's Hill looking down on the Forks.

To their right the road fell in beside a clear, turbulent river below—the Allegheny—then wound downhill between a few ghostly chimneys, where cabins had been burned out in an Indian rising. From their left the placid brown Monongahela surged into view. The Point was where the two streams met—met but did not yet mingle, for they flowed on awhile side by side, the clear and the muddy—to form the mighty Ohio.

"So that's Pittsburgh," Sukey said. "Not much to see, is there? For all the trouble it caused."

"No, not much."

In the wedge of land at the Point stood star-shaped Fort Pitt, pronged with bastions. Everything about it looked dilapidated and deserted, the brickwork stripped away, the gate sagging open, the epaulement crumbling into the moat. Along the Allegheny rows of fruit trees had been planted, and a large garden laid out. Two short streets of log houses and makeshift storehouses along the Monongahela seemed busy enough, too, and laden bateaux and pirogues were drawn up on the banks near a tethered line of pack ponies. West of the Allegheny, a line of humped wigwams marked an Indian encampment.

It was hard to think that only nineteen years before

—the year Harry was born and Sukey barely turned four—just about everybody in the whole world had heard of that place and those three rivers.

That was 1754 when the French laid claim to the Forks, and the English told them they couldn't have it. The two great empires fought, and half the civilized world—their allies—with them. And in the end, because they had tried to hold the Forks, the French had been driven from the New World.

(Harry was vague about exactly how it had started. Some young guffin of a militia officer mucked up his orders, brought on an engagement, and blundered them into a general war—that's what he'd heard. What was the youngster's name now? It had once been on every lip. Warrington? Washburn? Something like that. Militia indeed! Harry had served in the Regulars and had no use for amateur soldiers.)

And now the tide of war and fame had passed Pittsburgh by, leaving this placid, roughhewn settlement on the fringe of the civilized world. A gateway to the frontier. A funnel through which flowed trade with the Indians and long hunters probing as far as the Illinois country and settlers taking up the newly opened lands.

Harry gave himself a shake. All that was past. He and Sukey were concerned with their hope-filled future.

"We'd best get the cart, I reckon," he said. "Only the one last hill."

2
Greenhorn

At a crossroads at the foot of the last hill, Harry and Sukey paused, uncertain, and Harry set down the cart.

"We're going to stay in a tavern," Sukey insisted, and her tone implied that he'd suggested something different. "We agreed—a two-day rest when we reached the Forks."

"I'm not saying no, Sukey. But it's early yet—three full hours till sundown. Best to be getting the cart repaired."

Yes, that made sense to her. "But I'd better come with you, Harry. You're too soft-hearted. You'll let the smith overcharge you."

Harry felt his heels dig in and stubbornness harden in his veins, the way it always did when his sister tried to run him. "No," he said levelly. He picked up the handles of the cart and turned up the road toward the settlement. "You run on ahead and hire us a bed. Semple's Tavern—that's the best place in Pittsburgh. Right along the Monongahela, two-story building. And tell Mr. Semple, if he has the makings for supper, we'd like that too, please."

She smiled at this lordly order. Wilderness innkeepers, as they both knew, did you a favor taking you in at all. But she made no more objections to his handling the business with the blacksmith. "I'll get us lodging and food," she promised and set off down the muddy lane that called itself Market Street.

Harry watched a moment. His sister was tall and long-legged like him and had a fine, free-swinging stride that showed she was proud of her strong, womanly body and healthy good looks. She was garbed in coarse homespun dyed the drab yellow-brown they called butternut. Her moccasins and skirt hems were muddy from fording countless creeks and runs and marshes, her hair escaped from under her cap in uncombed tangles, and her shawl hung torn from briars and snags. But no one could say she wasn't a treat for the eyes, and Harry was proud of her. He might not need much else with which to conquer the wilderness as long as he had Sukey.

When she vanished behind a group of traders, Harry went on up Second Street and turned into Ferry. But the blacksmith shop wasn't where he had thought it was, and as he was looking around, his eye fell on a man lounging against the corner of a log building.

"Look here," Harry said, "can you direct me to the blacksmith's shop?"

He was a burly, short-necked man with a round face and jet black eyes. He looked Harry over, cart, bedraggled farmer's clothes, and all, with insolent tolerance. "Well, well, what we got here—another greenhorn?"

Harry couldn't very well deny the charge, so he cautiously said, "Uh—reckon so."

"Plan to take up lands hereabouts, do you?"

"Yes."

"Ain't you skeered of the redskins?"

"Well, I was hoping—"

"Where you from"—the stranger jerked his head vaguely toward the mountains—"the East?"

"That's right—Lancaster County."

"Lancaster County!" The stranger spat eloquently into the mud. It was plain what he thought of greenhorns from east of Susquehanna.

He was no greenhorn, that was obvious. His bottom half was encased in the moccasins and leggings—mere tubes of deerskin, actually, with the extra edges sliced into fringe—of an Indian, but from the thighs up he wore what every frontiersman wore—a hunting shirt. A linsey-woolsey frock it was, reaching halfway to the knees, broadly overlapping in front and with a belt tied around at the back. Over this he wore a short cape of some kind of hide, fringed with knotted yarn, and on his head an old cocked hat with a turkey feather stuck jauntily through a crack in the crown. He was armed to the teeth, of course—like everyone west of Susquehanna, it seemed to Harry—with bullet bag, powder horn, scalping knife, tomahawk, and rifle.

"Well?" Harry prodded. "The smith—where can I find him?"

For answer, the stranger strolled over to Harry's rig and circled it, taking his time, displaying as much contempt as he could manage. Then with a sudden movement, he jerked up the cover of the cart and peered frankly at its contents. He couldn't very well miss the biggest item the Warrilows owned.

"A pot still," he said, his eyes flicking expressionlessly at Harry. "You one of them no 'count Irishers?"

"No, but I learned—"

"*And* the squeezin's, well, well."

Before Harry could stop the man, he'd pulled out the telltale brown jug, extracted its corncob cork, and swung it to his shoulder with a practiced finger. Head turned sideways, he took a large swig.

But he paid for his greed, because Harry's whiskey, though smooth as oil, packed a monumental kick. The man's Adam's apple had barely bobbed before he was convulsed with a shudder. His eyes popped halfway out of his head, his shoulders rattled, and he burst out, "Kaaaaaa!" He wiped his mouth, swallowed a couple of times to assure himself that he was still able to, blinked, and blinked some more. Then, eyes still watering, he held the jug at arm's length and surveyed it with respect.

"That there's a hearty brew, greenhorn. Do your own 'stillin'?"

"Yes," said Harry, grinning to himself. "My master back East, he had an old Ulster Scot working for him, and Hector showed me. Said it was the easiest way to take grain to market."

"Wal, I reckon even a Lancaster farmer's bound to be right oncet in a while."

Harry had never done any distilling before Hector Craig taught him the craft, but once started, he found he had a natural gift. He had sold the whiskey back East as fast as he could buy jugs to bottle it, and he looked to do the same thing here.

The still was really why they had had to come afoot, for the money for a horse or ox had gone instead to the Lancaster coppersmith who made it. Sukey had argued for the horse. "We can live without a cash crop," she had said. "Later maybe we can get a still."

"I don't want us just to live—I want us to prosper. I admit that it's looking pretty much a long way into the future. But in the end, we'll be better off buying the still."

His long-range view had prevailed, and whiskey was to be their cash crop.

"Sour mash?" the stranger pursued.

"No, sweet mash."

"Double distilled?"

"Of course. But about the smith—?"

"Tell you what, greenhorn. You hand over a pint of this here brew, and I'll take you to the smith my own self."

Harry was about to agree wearily, but then his sister's voice echoed in his ears: *You're too soft-hearted. You'll let yourself be cheated.*

He snatched back the jug and stowed it in the cart. "I

don't see why I should. There are plenty of people to ask. I could find it myself with a little walking."

The frontiersman glared and let his hand rest for a moment on the tomahawk in his belt. But he must have decided that it wasn't worth scrapping over, because presently he shrugged and barked a short laugh. "All right, greenhorn. Follow me, it's jest down here."

He set off down Ferry Street toward the Monongahela, but after three strides he paused and held out a thick and grimy paw. "Name's Girty. Simon Girty."

"Oh? Pleased to meet you, Mr. Girty. I'm Harry Warrilow." Hastily he drew the cover back over his and Sukey's meager belongings and picked up the cart handles.

"That there all you own?" Girty said sneeringly. "Ain't much for a fam'ly to be settin' up on new lands."

Harry started to say, "There's just my sister and me," but something about the short-necked Mr. Girty made him hesitate to admit weakness. "We have more goods upriver," he lied warily. "This is only extras, like."

The other half-smiled—knowingly, Harry thought—and resumed his stride.

How much would the smithing cost? Harry wondered, as he trundled along in Girty's wake. Sukey had charge of their money, and he wasn't certain how much they had left. Suppose Sukey had already committed them to spending that at Semple's? Well, he'd have to chance it. Maybe the smith would take whiskey for his payment.

Ferry Street was a muddy lane of shanties, sheds, work yards, and horse lines. Here and there Harry saw evidence of a trader's establishment—stacks of hides and bales of trade goods awaiting shipment, bateau men loading up for a trip down the Ohio, clerks bustling in and out, and an occasional Indian, stolid in blanket and feathers, haggling over his stash of beaver. They passed one or two substantial houses which, though built of the usual squared logs, were nevertheless plainly the homes of rich men. When a clerkly looking gentleman, in a snuff-colored coat and on his head a tricorne, emerged from one such house, Girty flicked a finger at his forehead and intoned, "Aft'noon, Jedge." To Harry, he added when the man had nodded and passed on, "Mac-Kay. Jest been made magistrate for this here whole county of Westmoreland."

Everyone seemed to know Girty. A stout girl wearing a yoke from which hung two milk buckets paused before selling a dipperful to flash him a coquettish smile. Two ragged and grubby urchins followed them down the street, aping the frontiersman's stride. Any number of tall, lean buckskins, long rifles cradled in the crooks of their arms, drawled solemnly, "Howdy, Si . . ."

"Are you a trader?" Harry asked, idly curious.

"Nope. I'm the 'terpreter."

"Interpreter? Of what?"

"Injun. Delaware and Shawnee. Little Seneca."

Harry glanced at Girty more closely, impressed. "How did you learn to talk Indian? Did you—uh—live with them for a while?"

"Yep. Four years. Carried off in '54."

They reached the Monongahela riverfront, and Girty turned left. "Water Street," he said briefly.

The muddy lane dropped off on one side to the placid brown water, where the traders' boats were beached. At the corner was a work yard flanked on one side by a sprawling, squared-log house and on the other by the smithy. Above the door of the latter hung a sign: "A. MacBain, Ironwork and General Smithing." A banked fire glowed in the forge, and a deerhide apron hung from a doornail, but there was no sign of A. MacBain himself.

Girty dislodged his disreputable hat to scratch the back of his head. "Where's Anse got to this time of day?" he muttered. Then, cupping hands around his mouth, he bellowed, "Be-e-elle! Where the hell are you, you black witch?"

A small Negro woman, neatly dressed in blue drugget short gown and fresh white cap, appeared at the door of the house, arms akimbo. "What you want, you no 'count Girty?"

"What you think I want? Where's Anse?"

"Mist' Anse, he step hisself out."

"Will he be back?"

She glowered, vastly displeased. "Mist' Anse, he don't ax me can he or can't he. How I know does he come back or don't he?"

Eventually, however, she admitted that her master had stepped out for a nip at Ormsby's tavern, two doors over.

They left the cart in the work yard and returned to the street, Girty muttering about uppity darkies. There, right in front of them, was a creaking wooden sign, prominently displayed: "J. Ormsby, Lodging and Victuals, Ferry to Coal Hill." And as they took their first step toward it, Sukey appeared from the other direction.

"Sukey!" Harry called in surprise, but he was drowned out by Girty's much louder "There he is! *Anse!*"

Two men had emerged from the tavern, and as Sukey stepped forward to enter it, one of them put his arm across the doorway, blocking her path. "Wal, now, who is this here pretty lady?" he wondered aloud. Harry thought to himself, That's the *last* way to approach my sister!

"*Anse!* Hey, Anse!"

But the two were intent on Sukey, who said something haughty to them.

"Oh, see here, pretty lady, you wouldn't take yourself off afore we have a chance to feast our poor old eyes, now would you?"

"*Let . . . me . . . pass. . . .*"

"Why, Pittsburgh don't hardly *ever* see a lady's pretty as you, ma'am. Lookee here," he observed genially to his companions, "all flushed up in the face, pinklike. I declare, I ain't—"

At which point, Sukey grabbed the tomahawk from the man's belt and, using the handle, whacked his arm down. She then dropped the hatchet to the ground, stepped around him, and disappeared into Ormsby's without another word.

The other burst into a roar of laughter, slapping his companion on the shoulder, while he, nursing his damaged arm, gazed after Sukey. "I admire a lady to have spunk," he said, still grinning. But when Girty called his name for the third time and he glanced in their direction, the grin seemed to Harry a bit fake.

"Stop fool-playin' with ever' wench come to town and git to your proper work," Girty grumbled. "I got you a customer here. Wants some repairs to his handcart."

"Handcart, eh?" The smith strolled over, his grin widening into a savage leer. "Greenhorn farmer?" He pretended to sniff. "There's pigsty on him, right enough."

Harry braced himself to be looked over with the vast contempt that Pittsburghers reserved for newcomers. By way of defense, he examined the smith as closely as the smith was examining him. He was struck by how much he looked like Girty. Both had thick black hair and snapping black eyes and yet were fair complexioned. Both were husky, shoulders straining the cloth of their shirts. Both were about the same age—thirty, thirty-one. But MacBain was taller, longer, straighter—as though someone had taken Girty and stretched him lengthwise—and he had a kind of gloss lacking in the dingy interpreter. His hair fell into natural waves and glinted freshly, as though it saw a comb now and then, and where the back part was confined in a queue, the lower end fell into a corkscrew curl. He was not without a few blacksmithly smudges, but on the whole he lacked that untended and unwashed look that hovered over Girty. Moreover, though he wore a hunting shirt, he also wore decent breeches, woolen stockings, and sturdy cowhide shoes. "Respectable" was the word that came to Harry's mind. He wouldn't have dreamed of applying it to Simon Girty.

But respectable or not, it was soon apparent that the smith shared Girty's notion that greenhorns were fair game. "Handcart, eh? Too no 'count to own a horse, even. What's the valley comin' to, that's what I want to know."

"It's the wheel, Mr. MacBain," Harry said evenly. He'd be switched if they were going to get a rise out of him. "The metal tire is worn and beginning to pull off."

"The tire is worn. You hear? Don't even own a decent *hand*cart."

"He's from Lancaster County," Girty put in, joining the fun.

"Worse and *worse*. One of them Dutchies, I reckon. What's your name, boy?"

"Warrilow. Harry Warrilow."

"That don't sound Dutch to me. I reckon the Krauts run him right on out, and now he looks to honor *us* with his presence."

"We left the cart in your yard. Will you take a look?"

"He left the cart in my yard. You hear, Charlie? This greenhorn comes through the mountains with a ugly old broken-down cart, and then reckons Anse MacBain'll make it all new agin."

Harry saw that there was no point in going on as though he were getting straight responses. The smith would simply repeat what he said with a twist. Should he hold his tongue and wait out the ragging, or attack?

Through the tavern window he caught a glimpse of Sukey talking to the innkeeper. He wondered what she was doing there. She'd set out for Semple's. Was Semple's full up? Or prices too high? Hang it, the Warrilows weren't doing very well for themselves in Pittsburgh, and that was a fact. He decided to follow Sukey's example and attack.

"Look here, Mr. MacBain," he said, breaking into the middle of yet another jibe, "every man likes a joke and all, but just because a lady snubs you, that gives you no call to take it out on me. If you can't fix my cart, say so and be done with it."

It was the right move. The smith slowly grinned—a real grin this time, displaying big white teeth. "All right," he said after a minute, "let's see this here cart."

Five minutes later, back in the smithy, he surveyed the empty, bottom-up cart with a thoughtful scowl. "Felloe's loose. That's your real trouble. Put a fresh tire on, and it'll work loose again."

Harry felt his heart sink. "You mean, it can't be fixed?"

"Oh, it can be *fixed*. Cost you a pound."

A pound! They were counting their money in pennies! "Will you take whiskey instead? It's good stuff—ask Mr. Girty."

The smith got to his feet. "Well, Si?"

"I've tasted better," Girty growled.

Harry handed the jug to MacBain. "Try it for yourself then."

The smith slung the jug and sipped cautiously. Even so, it must have given his insides a jolt, for he said, "Haa-ah!" and shook his head with a snap.

"Not a bad old brew, greenhorn. Tell you what—a quart, and the job's done."

So they struck a bargain and shook on it, and the smith set to work with hammer and pry, getting the old iron off the rim. Working away, he said idly, "Got here jest in time for the weddin', greenhorn."

"What wedding?"

"The Armstrong girl and the Wallace boy."

"Who are they?"

"It don't matter who they are—they're gettin' married, so they's goin' to be a feast. Day after tomorrow."

"Don't you have to be invited?"

The smith paused in his work, then began to laugh uproariously. "Invited? You hear that, Si—invited."

The two laughed on and on and were joined by the smith's striker. Evidently the frontier considered invitations to be effete. He and Sukey would have to change their eastern ways of thinking, to adjust to this new way of life.

But in the meantime he had grown tired of abuse and insults. "Yes, invited," he said grimly. "I'm only asking for

information. Where I come from, they don't laugh at
strangers for not knowing local customs."

The smith stopped laughing. "They's sense in that, Si,"
he said as the other continued to guffaw.

"And where I come from," Harry went on, turning to
Girty, "we don't expect to be paid for giving directions,
either."

The laughter died in the burly frontiersman, and he
turned a dark, sullen red. "We don't like greenhorns
tellin' us what to do," he said threateningly.

"I'm not telling you what to do. I'm only telling you the
way decent people act."

"You callin' me not decent?"

"If the shoe fits, put it on."

"Mister, iffen you wants a fight, I'm game," Girty said
hoarsely. His little black eyes glittered, and his hand
strayed toward his tomahawk.

I've hit him where it hurts! Harry exulted inwardly.
And then, because in the Army you were taught to put
your enemy to flight and keep him that way, he added, "It
seems to me you could use a few lessons in proper
manners."

"By gorries, I'll take your scalp right now!"

Before the tomahawk was halfway out of Girty's belt,
the smith had stepped between them. "Put that dad-
blamed hatchet away, Si Girty! You ain't in no Shawnee
village now."

"He thinks he's better'n me!"

"What iffen he does? He ain't nothin' but a greenhorn
farmer. Now you git out of here."

"Let me crease him jest the oncet. Learn him who he's
dealin' with."

"Out!" said the smith. "I don't hold with no brawlin' and scrappin' on my propitty, and that means you. And you, too, greenhorn," he added with a stabbing glance at Harry.

Girty edged sullenly toward the street, casting hate-filled looks at Harry. "Dumb, pig-keepin' farmer," he growled. "Ain't even got him a rifle. Give him a year afore he starves hisself out or the Injuns gits his womenfolk."

"Go on!" said MacBain. "Go git you a gill of rum at Ormsby's. Take the pizen out of you."

When Girty had slouched off, still muttering, MacBain rounded on Harry. "Now, lookee here, greenhorn, let me give you some powerful good advice. You steer clear of the Girtys, hear? And when you can't steer clear, you keep your mouth shut."

"Girtys? There's more than one?"

"Four all told—plus a half brother and a mother. The boys was Injun-reared, and they come out with all the faults of Injuns and all the faults of whites, and not much of any kind of virtue. Bone idle, the lot of them, and shiftless and no 'count and pizen mean. Always sp'ilin' for a fight, that there's the Girtys, and when they fight, it's no holds barred, eye gougin' a specialty. And Simon's the worst of the lot, 'cause on top of ever'thin', he's vain as a turkey cock."

Harry didn't much cotton to being bawled out like a schoolboy—he'd had enough of that in the Army. "So you let them do what they please, is that it? Because they're meaner than anyone else?"

"No, that ain't it. But we stay out of their way as much as we can, and if we let them rile us, it's over somethin' worth a few bruises. You understand me, greenhorn?"

"I reckon," Harry said sullenly. "But for someone so

almighty dangerous, he walked out of here meek enough."

"He ain't afraid of me," MacBain declared. "He behaves hisself good for me, 'cause hereabouts ever'body got to keep on the right side of the smith. But they ain't a thing in the world Simon is skeert of—or any other Girty neither. You remember that, greenhorn."

He was turning away to resume work on the spoke when something caught his eye and transfixed it. "Why, pretty lady," he said, his face lighting up. "Wal, now, if this here ain't a honor to my place of business!"

Harry looked around. There stood Sukey in the smithy doorway, directing a murderous glare at the smith.

3
Anse

Still glaring, Sukey darted to Harry's side, slipped her arm possessively around his waist, and hugged him tight. "How dare," she said, "how *dare* you insult my brother?"

The smith's face took a rapid turn for the worse. "Your—?" He glanced at Harry in shock.

"It's all right, Sukey," Harry said.

"It's *not* all right!" She stamped her foot. "Who does this—this oaf think he is?"

"Mr. MacBain is the smith. He's fixing our broken wheel."

"And I suppose name-calling is his way of treating all his customers!"

It felt good to have someone on his side, but Harry had had a change of heart in the last few minutes, and he thought now that the smith was right. Why pick a senseless fight with a stranger—or let him pick one with you? There were enough things on the frontier that you *had* to fight over.

"Mr. MacBain—well, he was giving me some advice, Sukey. Pretty good advice, I reckon."

"And the rough side of his tongue into the bargain. Well, it doesn't surprise *me!* Any man who'd put himself into a woman's path on the public street wouldn't think twice about what he'd do or say to a man!"

The smith's natural self-possession came back to life, and he took an undaunted step toward the Warrilows. With a rude but jaunty bow, he introduced himself formally: "Andrew MacBain, ma'am, at your service."

"At my service indeed!"

"But you can call me Anse if you take the notion. You, too, guh—" He had started to say "greenhorn" and only caught the word as it was tumbling from his tongue.

Harry grinned to himself and took pity on the man. "I'm Harry Warrilow, and this is my sister Susannah."

"Most happy to meet up with you, Miss Susannah."

She regarded him stonily until Harry nudged her. Then she dropped the smallest possible curtsy. *"Mr.* MacBain. Come, Harry, I have lodgings for us."

"You and the pretty lady go ahead," the smith said, all smiles. "You can leave your things here while you get yourself set for the night."

"Thanks. Yes, shall we go Sukey?"

While MacBain escorted them gallantly to the door of the smithy, Sukey sailed out with her nose in the air. In the street, she said, "Really, Harry! You do take up with the most—the most *awful* people!"

"But he's the only smith in town. And I had to get the cart repaired."

But this explanation went in one ear and out the other as she scolded away. Anse MacBain had committed two capital sins: He had played the brash ladykiller with

Sukey, and he had bawled Harry out. Sukey might have forgiven the former, especially since MacBain seemed to have changed his tone considerably, but not for yelling at her little brother. Harry was his sister's ewe lamb, her heart's darling, and she would not tolerate the smallest slight put upon him by anyone—anyone but herself.

"I think he's sweet on you," Harry ventured when she momentarily ran out of breath.

"From someone like that, it's not a compliment."

"He's not such a bad sort, Sukey. He's repairing the wheel for a quart of whiskey—a dirt-cheap bargain."

"Oh, I've heard enough about the creature!" she cried with a cross flap of her hand. "Come on, our lodgings are down this way." And they started off through the bustling street.

Considering its size—just four little blocks of houses —Pittsburgh was a crowded place. Traders pushed into town, leading strings of pack ponies piled high with pelts and kegs of potash. Others, their animals carrying kettles, powder, blankets, matchcoats, trinkets, copper wire, rum, waited at the Allegheny ferry landing to start their journeys into the Ohio country. Families arrived by boat down the Monongahela or by horseback from the Braddock road and camped above the town. Bearded hunters just back from the Illinois country stood on street corners and stared at passersby from gaunt, dirty faces. Indians strolled the streets by twos and threes, crowding into traders' stores to jabber in their strange tongue and pick over the goods on display or visiting the smithy to have their guns repaired.

Harry took it all in wonderingly as Sukey led him out Ferry Street to a small, squared-log building on a corner.

"This is Charles Richard's tavern," she said. "It's the only one we can afford."

Mr. Richard was a free Negro, and though the place was barren enough, it was clean and tidy and inviting. The smells drifting up from the kitchen made Harry realize how hungry he was for something besides johnnycake. They were given a bucket of well water and directed to the garret floor where, in a corner under the slanting roof, they were to sleep. Harry left his sister there to wash her feet and face and comb out her hair, and returned to the smithy. Re-tiring a wheel wasn't something that happened every day, and Harry didn't want to miss it.

By then MacBain had fitted the wheel together and was at work welding a fresh piece of iron over the broken patch. He held the metal across the anvil with a pair of tongs and indicated with a small hammer where he wanted his striker to hit with the sledge *tink . . . clang . . . tink . . . clang . . . tink . . . clang. . . .* The glowing lump of metal flattened out, slowly cooling to yellow and then ash gray. When the weld was complete, the smith measured the inside of this repaired tire with a wheeled tool, then double-checked it against the outer rim of the wooden wheel. Considering that the wheel had to be slightly larger than the rim, the mended tire measured right on the button.

Harry whistled, impressed. It took no small skill to know just how much metal to allow for a weld. "You have a real touch," he said, openly admiring.

The smith grinned. "All right now, Charlie, over to the forge with it. Maynard! Maynard! Belle, where'n blazes is that boy of your'n? Dad-blame it!"

The two men had gotten the tire to the forge for reheating when a little Negro boy of about ten put in an

appearance—a spidery child, all long thin arms and legs and neck—and scuttled over to work the bellows. "Not that now. Fetch water, Maynard. Fill up that there tub. Hop to it. We'll need it in a few minutes."

"Yessir, Mist' Anse."

Thin or not, Maynard was a tough youngster, handling the heavy wellsweep with ease. It took the metal half an hour to heat up thoroughly, and by then he had managed to fill the tub. "I done it, Mist' Anse," he announced. "See there."

"Good boy. Now stand clear."

It was the supreme moment. With tongs, the smith and his striker, one on either side, lifted the reheated tire from the forge fire—a glowing hoop of cherry red—and carried it over to where the wheel lay waiting. The heat had expanded the iron, but even so, it barely fitted over the wheel. The men had to ram it into place with hammers. Smoke sizzled up from the scorched wood. The men sprinkled water on the iron, then dropped it into Maynard's tub. A cloud of steam rose, hissing and bubbling, the water boiled, and there was a loud *pop!* from the new spoke, driven home in its joint when the cooling iron shrank tight around the wheel. A few minutes later, when it was cool enough to handle with the bare hand, MacBain drove nails in around the rim and pronounced the job done.

With the wheel back on the cart, Harry reloaded it. "Get me something to measure out, Mr. MacBain, and I'll give you your whiskey."

"Call me Anse," said the smith. "And don't bother none 'bout the whiskey." He grinned oddly at Harry, his teeth very white in his sooty face. "You just present this here job to Miss Susannah with my compliments."

"I don't understand. We made a bargain. You more than earned it, Mr. MacBain. Sukey wouldn't want me to accept it for nothing."

"Anse. Get used to callin' me Anse."

"Well, Anse then."

"And I couldn't take no kind of payment from my future brother-in-law. There, now, can't say I never warned you none."

Harry stood without moving for a good minute and a half. A streak of jealousy had shot through him as red hot as that metal hoop had been a few moments ago.

"Oh, no, you don't!" he wanted to shout into the smith's smug face. "Sukey belongs to *me!*"

His feelings surprised him. Oh, he loved his sister, naturally. Each was all the other had, and they were close. But he had gotten used to being somewhat more loved than loving, of taking Sukey's affection for granted. Now here was this grinning blacksmith threatening to take her away, and for some reason it seemed possible.

He drew a breath finally and said, "Oh?"

"Yep. Oh."

"You're off to a bad start, you know." It was only with effort that he kept his voice from creaking.

"Bad start's only a bad start."

"You won't help yourself any by not taking payment, Mr. MacBain. Sukey won't like your thinking she can be bought."

"Call me Anse," he said, still grinning. "And you tell Miss Susannah that hereabouts we help each other out. It don't do for a body to turn down a neighbor's offer of a helpin' hand. It's notional."

Troubled and still raging with jealousy, Harry was forced to accept that arrangement. He put back the canvas cover and picked up the cart handles. It certainly worked much better now. "Thank you anyway. It was a fine job."

"You're dad-blamed right it was a fine job. Oh, and, Harry?"

"Yes?"

"I seen you and Miss Susannah ain't got much by way of goods to be settin' up with. You load up my coal bin for me, and I'll make you a few things."

"Load up?"

"Across the Mon. Coal Hill. Got me a pit there."

In spite of himself, Harry brightened. They had come badly equipped, it was true. Partly that had been because of weight, partly because of poverty.

"Have you also got a boat?"

"Ever'body in Pittsburgh's got a boat."

"We'd meant to leave day after tomorrow."

"Put it off another day. You want to stay for the weddin' anyway."

His real reason is wanting to see Sukey again, Harry thought. Still, there were so many things they needed. "All right, Mr. MacBain," he agreed reluctantly. "I'll haul some tomorrow."

"There's just one thing: You got to start calling me Anse."

Harry left the smithy and trundled the cart back to Mr. Richard's, where Sukey was waiting. Mr. Richard rang a cowbell to announce that supper was ready. Men began to push in from the street and the yard outside, shoving and elbowing for places at the big plank table. It filled most of the space on the ground floor and was surrounded by stools and benches of puncheon—logs split in half with the flat side up. By the time the first steaming bowls and wooden platters were carried in, eaters were packed elbow to elbow clear around it—traders, a settler in Pittsburgh on some errand, bearded trappers, two Indians, other rough and noisy nondescripts. Sukey and Harry managed

to get seats at one corner, where there was a little room to move, and prepared to eat heartily.

The meal started with a gigantic Allegheny River pike—fifteen pounds if it weighed an ounce and enough to feed everyone at the crowded table. Then stewed squirrel, ham, proper baked cornbread with butter, a large cheese, a kind of pumpkin bread, an egg dish, and as much cider as they could hold. Blissful, Harry ate and ate and ate, feeling his stomach expand warmly. How good food was! Sukey had been right to insist on their having their treat. The meal put new heart and spirit into him.

Around him there was hardly a sound that wasn't a chomp or a slurp. Mrs. Richard and her daughters bustled to and fro, handing around trenchers and noggins, dipping up cider, cutting bread. Mr. Richard took his place by the rum keg near the door and made flip for those customers who could pay extra.

Then as men left the table, the pace slowed, and a few turned curiously toward the Warrilows. Finally one opened: "Y'all takin' up new lands, stranger?" He spoke to Harry, but his eyes were on Sukey. Everyone's were—she was the only woman at the table.

Too weary and full for another session of banter, Harry admitted that he was indeed planning to settle.

"Jest in from the East, are you?"

"Yes."

"Well, what's the news? They still goin' on 'bout that there tea tax?"

"After a fashion, but a lot of the excitement has died down."

"Some folks 'round here, they thinks Americans ought to be independent. Git out from under them Parliament people for good."

"Independent?" First Harry was shocked, then amused. "Why, how could Americans survive without the government back home? Like a body without a head."

"Make up our own head. Make up our own laws, too."

Harry laughed. Five years before, when he had first come over with his regiment, there had been a lot of rioting and unrest. But it had all petered out, and you hardly ever heard of radicals like Sam Adams and James Otis anymore. "And choose your own king, I reckon," he said, rising. "Come on, Sukey. Let's go for a walk before bed."

He had had no chance, earlier, to tell her what had happened at MacBain's on his second visit. He told her now, and as he had expected, she was angry over the smith's refusal to accept payment.

"Oh, Harry!" she cried. "How could you let him put shame on me that way?"

"Well, he says frontier people have to help each other, that we have to learn to give and take from strangers."

She made an exasperated, tongue-clicking noise and jammed her fists into her waist. Rather pleased with that reaction, Harry went on to explain about MacBain's offer of work. She stared at him, her expression unchanged. Then she said grimly, "The trouble with being poor is that *everyone* can do you favors, and you can't turn them down."

"Yes," he said—he had had the same first reaction himself—but his heart lightened. "We won't always be poor, though. When we have our farm going, we won't be beholden to *anybody*."

"How much will he pay you?"

"He offered to make us some tools."

"He saw how little we have, I suppose."

"Well, yes, the cart had to be emptied."

She took his arm, still angry but beginning to see the good side of it. "Oh, I suppose it's all for the best. Let's walk up the hill."

They climbed up the path down which they had come a few hours earlier, enjoying the freedom of not having the cart to tote, the pleasure of stretched-full stomachs, the relief of having arrived at their first goal. Over the top of Grant's Hill, a full moon had risen in the blue-gray twilight sky. Sukey smiled to see it, and Harry felt a sudden pang. She *is* a pretty lady, he thought. Any man would want her.

He brushed his fears aside. MacBain was his own worst

enemy. Everything he had done so far had turned Sukey further against him.

"Well, we're in Pittsburgh," she said, surveying the settlement below them, "and that's a good bit all by itself."

"Right," he said. He did not tell her what else MacBain had said. He would save that for the next time he felt he might lose her.

4

A Wedding in Town

The night was less pleasant for Harry than the meal. After so many weeks of sleeping on the ground, which could always be hollowed out a bit to fit the human spine, boards felt hard and unyielding under his back. He woke up with his hair hurting. Even so, he was happy enough to rise at dawn, eat another hearty meal, and report to MacBain for work.

Hauling coal turned out to be hard, exasperating labor. Harry had to row across the Monongahela, beach the boat under the towering cliff that faced the Point, and scramble up the steep path to the coal mines.

These were shallow holes cut into the face of the slope and marked with the names of the owners—or, rather, lessees. For the Penns had lotted out Coal Hill and rented plots to anyone who wanted to mine the surface coal. The forge being a hungry consumer of fuel, MacBain had two mines, and Harry attacked them by turns.

When he had enough of the crumbly, dusty material to

fill his three hempen sacks, he would throw them downhill, skid and plunge after them, load them in the boat, and row back to Pittsburgh.

By the end of the day, he had managed to fill MacBain's huge coal bin. And the smith, serious about his side of the bargain, had forged them a number of useful items: a broadax for squaring timbers, hinges, a latch, a reaping sickle, nails, a great fireplace crane for Sukey, a bake kettle.

He was a fast worker, and everything that came off his anvil had a kind of natural grace. To Harry's dismay, Sukey admired it too. "He does good work," she said grudgingly. "But all this is too much pay for one day's wages."

But she solved that problem with her usual directness. Early in the morning of their third day in Pittsburgh, she took the jug of whiskey to the smith's house and told his housekeeper, Belle, that she had come to pay a debt. MacBain was hard at work in the smithy at the time and had evidently not thought to warn Belle, for she smilingly accepted two quarts of whiskey.

"Now," Sukey said happily on her return, "let's get ready for the wedding."

It was being held at Semple's tavern, a large building of squared logs, with three rooms on the ground floor and a mahogany staircase that was the talk of Pittsburgh. Here the entire population of the village gathered at noon, to see the young couple married by Judge MacKay.

The ceremony over, everybody trooped out to the yard behind the tavern and the barn, where long puncheon tables were laden with hams, turkeys, cornbread, cakes, and many other bowls and platters of food.

Feeling shy, Harry and Sukey stood a little apart. Sukey had spent the previous day washing their clothes, so they were clean and presentable. But it took more than that to feel at home in this boisterous frontier crowd.

Harry peered about apprehensively for MacBain. The smith was not to be seen, but Simon Girty was. Turkey leg in one hand and noggin in the other and surrounded by four or five cronies, he roared with laughter as he stuffed himself. There'll be a fight before long, Harry thought, and resolved to stay well clear.

Then quite suddenly MacBain appeared, clean and resplendent. He whipped off his tricorne hat, held it out sideways, and, taking one step backwards, bowed from the waist. "Your servant, Miss Susannah ma'am."

It was a gesture that could not be ignored. Sukey's grip on Harry's forearm tightened convulsively. Then her fingers relaxed, and she dropped the smith an answering curtsy. She was just turning coolly away when MacBain said, "Can I help you to some food, Miss Susannah?"

"I'm with my brother. He'll get me what I need. Come, Harry."

But MacBain did not dismiss quite that easily. As he and Sukey headed for the food table, Harry found that the smith had fallen in on the other side of Sukey and was chatting away gaily, quite as if he had been invited.

Harry was ashamed of the quick anger and fear that flooded through him. You're plain selfish! he told himself roughly. She's twenty-three—it's long past time for her to marry! Why, she'd be far better off here in Pittsburgh than alone in the wilderness with you.

But shame didn't help much. He not only wanted her—wanted to keep her affection all for himself—but he plain needed her. He could never wrench a farm from the

wilderness without her help. So, it was an immense relief
to him when somebody came tugging at MacBain's sleeve
with word of emergency repairs most desperately needed,
and the smith had to hurry off.

Harry and Sukey filled trenchers with food and wooden
cups of cider and found a corner where they could sit.
"He means well, I suppose," Sukey said suddenly. "At
least he's mended his manners." Quite a space of time had
passed since MacBain had departed. He must have been
on her mind throughout it. A bad sign.

"Would you like to dance, Sukey?" Out in the barn, a
fiddle could be heard tuning up.

"It's too soon after eating for me. But you go ahead if
you like."

People were beginning to leave the food and stream out
to the threshing floor for the dancing. "I reckon I just
will," Harry said. "If you're sure you don't mind?"

"Quite sure."

Harry got rid of his trencher and cup and slipped in
with the others. A cart was stored at the back. He climbed
up and perched on the uptilted end, from which he could
get a good view of the festivities. Perhaps he would find a
girl and dance himself—later.

The fiddler, a middle-aged black man, and the dance
caller, a white man about the same age, stood on upturned
kegs, poised to begin. Young people formed up for a
square. One couple was the bride and groom, of course,
and the others seemed to be courting. They pitched into
the dance with yips and shouts, while the spectators
clapped and whistled and stamped and cheered them on.
The square over, they fell to jigging, two couples at a time.
When one couple gave up, exhausted, another couple
took their place, and this went on until the poor musician

brought his tune to a close, himself dripping with sweat.

Harry was caught up in the excitement of it by then and wanted to join in. He wasn't sure he could handle a square dance—he had never lived among people who danced in that fashion—but he was certain he could perform a reel with the best of them. His eye had fallen on a pert little maid of sixteen or so, with sandy hair and freckles.

He jumped down from the cart and made his way through the crowd to where the girl was sitting on a barrel top. "Do you reckon you'd care to be my partner for the reel, ma'am?" he asked her.

She batted her eyes at him flirtatiously. "Don't know as I'd feel up to it, stranger."

"Why, ma'am, you look to be light as a feather on your feet."

"We-ell, I don't rightly know," she stalled, wanting him to work on her a little. "My daddy, he don't like for me to have time for no strangers."

"I'm Harry Warrilow. There, now I'm not a stranger anymore."

The musician had finished his cider and wiped his mouth on his sleeve. There went the instrument to his chin, and here came the first notes of the "The Marquis of Huntly's Farewell."

"It's a reel," said Harry. "Come dance, do."

She went with him willingly enough, but as they were taking their places in the set, a beefy hand closed on Harry's arm. "That there is *my* girl!" Simon Girty growled in his ear. "And I don't cotton to no greenhorn walkin' in and layin' claim to my propitty."

He reeked of cider, and his little black eyes were veined with red, but he was still steady on his feet and dangerous. Harry glanced at the girl. "Well, ma'am? You prefer Mr. Girty?"

"*Mister* Girty!" she sniffed. "He don't own me none."

"Very well, let's not hold up the dance."

His heart was thumping hard as he shook free of Girty's grasp and went into the first figure of the reel. What was it MacBain had said? "Eye gouging a specialty." Harry shivered. As long as the dance went on, he was pretty sure to be safe, because Girty would turn the whole group against himself if he interrupted a dance. But when that was done, Harry was in big trouble.

Do-si-doing around his partner, he tried to smile at her reassuringly, but all the while he was aware of the murderous glare being directed at his back by the angry Girty.

He darted his eyes around, trying to pick out Sukey, but she must have been outside still. Not that it would help him to find his sister—he couldn't very well take refuge behind her skirts. Holding his partner's hands to slide down to the end of the set and back, he tried to think of a way out. Not a way out with honor or anything—just a way out. Suppose he simply refused to put up his fists?

Hang it, that's what he'd do. Let them call him a coward.

The set ended. He thanked the girl. She did not leave him, however, but hung onto his arm and sauntered with him up to Girty, who was leaning grimly against one of the roof supports. Clearly she enjoyed the notion that two men were going to scrap over her.

"By gorries, greenhorn, I'll have your front teeth for that. Outside. Git."

"I'm not going to fight you, Mr. Girty."

The man's mouth dropped open slightly. "You yellow?" he said after a minute.

"If you like."

"Well, I don't like!" he roared. People had begun to notice that a fight was in the making and gathered around enthusiastically. "You been askin' for a dustin' ever since you blew into town, and now I'm goin' to give you one. Ain't that right, folks?"

"Go git him, Si!" called one of his cronies, and there were cheers and laughter from the crowd.

For a moment, Harry debated his chances in a fight with Girty. He was cold sober and a couple of inches taller, and he'd done some brawling in his Army days. But Girty was at least fifty pounds heavier and had had years of practice at this sort of thing. And there was the eye gouging business.

"Not me," he said, folding his arms firmly. "I don't fight." Summoning all his resolution, he slipped past Girty and walked out of the barn. The party divided—the young and lighthearted went back to dancing, the sports and the local toughs followed Harry. Soon he and Girty were the center of an excited ring.

Most were jeering at him: "Coward . . . yellow belly . . . farmer. . . ." But not everyone. "Man has a right to choose," he heard someone say, and another voice added that a wedding was no place for a battle.

"They's bad blood atween him and me," Girty insisted. "He needs a good lesson, and they ain't no time better'n the present."

"I won't fight."

"You one of them no 'count Quakers?" Girty demanded.

"No. I just see no sense in fighting over nothing. If I fight, it's *for* something."

There was murmuring in the crowd. His refusal was beginning to win grudging respect. Even one of Girty's cronies offered a compromise: "Shootin' match? How 'bout makin' it a shootin' match?"

That brought a cheer from the crowd and an evil smile from Girty. "What say, greenhorn? Nothin' hard—jest that there tree down there, not more'n eighty yards."

"There's no point in that," he said. "I'm no marksman." Besides, he might have added, I have only an old smoothbore fowling piece.

The crowd, which had brightened up at the suggestion of the match, groaned with disappointment. "You ain't good for nothin', you ain't," Girty hooted.

"Not much," Harry agreed cheerfully. But as he did so, he had an idea. There *was* one thing he was good at—well, pretty good. "But if you want to make it a foot race, I'm game."

Girty pulled back, frowning, and hastily looked Harry over. He rubbed his bristly chin, and there was a long pause. "Come on, Si!" someone called impatiently. "Moment ago, you was all hot to get the stranger in a contest. Now he's offerin'."

"Where'd we run?" he asked.

Harry wanted to make it a good long run, because he had plenty of stamina and knew how to pace himself, and he stood a better chance of outlasting the burly Girty. Trouble was, there wasn't much level ground near Pittsburgh. "Well, we might start on the Forbes road—at that creek it crosses—on down to the crossroads, then back up here and finish at Hogg's Pond creek on the Braddock road."

"That there's over a mile."

"No sense not making a good contest of it."

The crowd nodded, agreeing: "Yep . . . aye . . . the lad's right."

Girty hemmed and hawed some more, then shrugged and said, "Done!" He held out a grimy paw for Harry to shake.

With a couple of others to act as starters, they set out for the Forbes road, Harry looking the ground over with care, to mark in his mind any spots where he would have to watch his footing. Now that he had at last embroiled Harry in a test of some kind, Girty was almost sunny tempered, laughing and joking with the starters. When they were nearly to their starting point, he turned to Harry.

"Fancy yourself as a runner, do you?"

"Well, not exactly. But I'm a whole lot better at running than at shooting."

"How 'bout somethin' ridin' on the race?"

"A bet, you mean? I've got nothing to bet with."

"You got your still."

Harry stopped dead and stared at the man. Girty's natural expression of craftiness had deepened to the point of desperate cunning. "The still is valuable," Harry retorted. "Why should I run the risk of losing it in some silly wager?"

"Wal, now, s'posin' I was to put this here up agin it?" And Girty held out his rifle.

Stunned, Harry took the weapon and examined it wonderingly. One of the most important items he was going to have one day was a rifle. He had not expected to get one for years and years, though, for they cost three times as much as a musket. Girty's was a beauty—nearly six feet long from its curly maple, brass-bound butt to the

tip of its octagonal barrel. All the care that he had not
bothered to apply to himself he had lovingly lavished on
the gun. The brass insets gleamed, the barrel was rustless
and unstained with powder burns, the hickory ramrod
polished.

Harry was tempted—oh, he was tempted. I'm pretty
fast, he argued with himself feverishly. And ten years
younger. And to have a rifle . . .

But with an effort he thrust the weapon back to Girty's
hands. "I can't," he said. "My sister is half owner of the
still. I've no business gambling with what isn't all mine."

"Your sister," Girty sneered. "Petticoat gov'ment. No
man lets a woman run him."

Most of Girty's jibes did not bother Harry, but that one
was so close to the truth that it stung. Because he knew
that Sukey, if consulted, would never have agreed to the
bet. Harry nodded angrily at the rifle. "Does the bullet
mold go with it?"

"It does," said Girty with a wolfish smile.

"Then you've got a wager, Mr. Girty." And for a second
time, they shook.

They arrived at the Forbes road creek, and the starters
marked a line in the dirt with their heels. Harry and Girty
lined up behind it. Harry stared down the long road in
front of him, trying to swallow the great lump in his
throat. His palms were sweating, his knees weak. What
have I done? he thought. Risked our whole future just
because of a jibe? After quarreling with Sukey, hauling
the still all this long way—to throw it away. . .

One of the starters raised his rifle to fire into the air.
Harry gave himself a mental shake. Regrets were useless.
What he had to do now was concentrate on the race. Pace

. . . pace . . . Don't let the leader get too far away, but save something for the final burst.

Crrck-ow . . . ow . . . ow . . .

Girty burst into motion, powerful legs churning away, powerful arms pumping. Harry was well behind before they'd gone ten paces. He drove himself to keep up, but the road ran downhill here, and he had to watch where he put his feet. Girty did not seem to need to, for he plunged recklessly into hollows and around boulders and quickly widened the distance between them. Wider and wider and wider. Dust smoked out behind him, making Harry cough, slowing him still further.

Where the ground leveled out, Harry speeded up a bit. Fright urged him to drive himself faster yet, faster, flat out. His legs twitched to be turned loose. He's fast—you made a bad guess about his speed. Hurry . . . catch him. . . .

He fought panic. No, no, forget about Girty. Think about the road. Pace yourself, save something.

Soon he began to feel the rhythm of his stride. He was running well. If it weren't for that stupid bet, he would be enjoying himself. Here was the public garden. Girty was nearly to the far end of it before Harry reached the near end. Pace . . . save. . . . There's a lot of race still to be run. He hasn't gained since we hit flat ground.

Girty was at the crossroads, turning onto the Braddock road. Was he beginning to flag? Harry pounded after him, reached the crossroads himself. Yes, they were definitely closer together now. And the uphill part of the race still lay ahead. Pace . . . save. . . .

Harry concentrated on his running, eyes on the road ahead. He was almost surprised when he found Girty in

his line of vision. The man *was* slowing up, and no mistake. The ground was beginning to rise now. Was that a stagger? It certainly looked—Yes, he was distinctly weaving now, his feet all over the road.

Still holding his stride, Harry passed Girty just as they hit Second Street, where the wedding guests were lined up, cheering. He had not yet gone into his finishing sprint and probably didn't need to. But he wouldn't for worlds miss the chance to make Girty look as bad as possible. With the creek in sight, he lengthened his stride—faster and faster and faster. He zipped across the finish line so fast that he could not stop himself from plunging into the creek.

The crowd was all around him, clapping him on the back, giving him three cheers. They seemed to think he had done something clever—tricked Girty into competing at a disadvantage—and they admired him for it. He was still heaving when Sukey broke through the crowd, flung her arms around him, and gave him one of her fierce hugs. "That's my Harry—you show them all!"

A few minutes later, breathless and wobbly, Girty dragged himself across the finish line to a chorus of hoots. He braced himself against a tree, panting like a dog. When he was somewhat recovered, he stalked off, but not before he'd given Harry a look. "This don't finish it atween you and me, Warrilow," he snarled as he passed.

But Harry hardly heard, for here, up the road, came the starters, carrying his new rifle.

5
Their Place

The following morning, they set out on the last leg of their journey to Olethey Creek. There was no road, only the Allegheny to guide them.

The first few miles, trundling the old cart through the woods, were easy enough. But then the ground began to get steeper and the woods thicker. Sometimes they had to make long detours around thick patches of growth. Other times Harry had to get out the felling ax and cut a path. They tried to hug the river, so they would not lose their way, but often they had to swing far inland to avoid a swamp or find a fording place.

The valley was beautiful. A deer drank at the water's edge and lifted his head to stare at them. A male mallard flew past them and settled on the surface near his mate and her flotilla of ducklings.

"Isn't the dogwood pretty!" Harry said. Now that he had Sukey out of MacBain's reach, he felt relaxed and happy.

"Yes," said Sukey and, ever practical, added, "The wood makes good weaving shuttles. Close grained."

How different this green and white setting was from the

gray November river he had traveled with Kaspar Wertmüller. Kaspar had accompanied Harry on his first trip to the Forks and helped him choose a site for the Warrilow farm. The Wertmüllers knew everything about farming, so Harry had eagerly accepted his offer. They had covered the Forbes road comfortably on Wertmüller's horses and then hired an Indian to ferry them up the Allegheny from Pittsburgh.

"Trees mit nuts ve must look for," Kaspar had explained earnestly. "Vere iss nuts iss goodt soil. And earth vot gifs *der Kalk. Der Kalk* makes in cows and horses strong bones. Undt landt mit goodt vater, falls down heffy—someday you vill make a mill. But near to riffer, so carry to market iss easy."

Even then, bleak with early winter, the winding, rushing river had seemed to Harry beautiful and full of promise, each tributary creek and stream lovelier than the last. They explored these side streams and their banks, but Kaspar was never satisfied. Not enough trees mit nuts. Not enough *der Kalk* (by which, Harry eventually discovered, he meant limestone). Too much falls down heffy. In the end, it was Harry who said, "This is it."

He had seen one patch of woods that was somehow different—different and infinitely beguiling. A sweet stretch of land cupped by rolling hills, where great sheets of grapevines blanketed the trees and wild raspberries grew riotously in every swatch of sun.

They had turned up one of the tributary creeks, which their guide called the Olethey, and had paddled for perhaps a mile when Harry's eye was caught by the little valley. A swift-flowing brook ran down the middle of it, and you could see crayfish along its edges. Harry loved the place at sight.

Kaspar looked it over critically. *Ja,* plenty trees mit nuts. *Ja,* a goodt stand of maples for sugar. *Ja,* brook iss goodt—goodt fall. Nein, not enough *der Kalk*—badt, badt. But up on hillside iss—iss *das Salzquelle!* In his excitement, Kaspar could not remember the English word, and it was all he could do to seize Harry and drag him up the hill through the trees and show him what he had found: a salt spring.

"Salt, salt," he babbled feverishly. "Iss nottingk more better—for men, for animals."

Harry had known from looking at the spot that this was Their Place. The discovery of the salt spring settled it for Kaspar, and together they marked out a tomahawk claim—blazed trees with hatchet chops along a rough boundary line—girdled trees for a clearing, and made a rude dugout in the side of a hill. The dugout was walled and floored with puncheon and would serve Harry and his sister as a temporary shelter while their cabin was abuilding. Then it was back to Pittsburgh and the return east to wait for spring.

Now, laboriously making way for the cart through the woods, Harry felt elation build up in him. In a few days now they'd be there—they'd be home.

They spent the first night of their journey camped by the mouth of a creek. Harry went out with the rifle and, by a bit of luck, came back with a rabbit for supper. He had been roundly scolded by Sukey, the day of the wedding, when she found out about the wager—"Harry, what if you'd *lost?*"—but she did like the meat he could provide with it.

No amount of practice would make him a real marksman, he was certain of that. The day of the wedding, after the foot race, some of the men had held a shoot-off, firing at a nail driven into a tree. No one was allowed to enter the contest who couldn't put five bullets out of five within a hand's span of the nail at eighty yards, and there were nevertheless at least thirty entrants. Harry would never be in that class, even if he could afford the powder needed for constant practice. But the new rifle made a marked difference in the number of times he came home emptyhanded.

He cleaned it as Sukey dished up rabbit stew. "This is going to make things a lot easier," he said.

"I suppose." She eyed the rifle. "But you've made an enemy—a bad enemy, I'm told."

"Well, we've left Girty behind in Pittsburgh, and Anse says—" He stopped. Anse? Drat the man!

"Yes?"

"Well, he says Girty is mean but also lazy. He'd take revenge if it was easy to do, but he won't put himself out to get back at me."

She did not reply, and Harry studied her face, trying to find a clue to her feelings about the smith. She had softened toward the man, no doubt about that. But that didn't mean she was bowled over. She certainly hadn't tried to postpone their leaving Pittsburgh. Why don't I just up and ask her? Harry wondered, but something kept him silent.

"Read the deed, please, Harry," she said when the meal was over, and he decided to take that as a good sign.

The second day it rained torrents, and they had to take shelter in the lee of a great outcrop of rock. Crouched there with nothing to do, Harry brooded. As the problems of Pittsburgh faded, he was becoming more acutely aware of those that lay ahead. For instance, how were they to raise their cabin?

He could cut and square off the logs by himself. But one man alone couldn't lift timbers over his head. That took a whole team. Most frontier folk took up new lands as part of a group. Or they moved only twenty or thirty miles from their relatives and friends, who would come in a body to help them. Harry and Sukey were quite alone.

There was a settlement of traders at Kittanning, not far from Their Place. But traders were notoriously hardened, cheating the Indians flagrantly and unconcerned with the problems of other whites. It wasn't likely they would help. Could he hire Indians? Probably not. They considered labor of this sort degrading, and, moreover, it distressed them to see the forest cut down. In any event he would have nothing with which to pay them until after his distilling next fall. He could, he supposed, return to Pittsburgh and enlist a crew, but again payment was a problem.

MacBain would be willing to help, of course, and doubtless could persuade others. No, no, Harry thought irritably.

"It's clearing up now," Sukey said. "Shall we go on a ways or stay the night here?"

"Let's go on. The sooner we get there, the sooner we'll get our first crop in."

"Good." She gave a gusty little sigh. "Oh, Harry, I can't wait till I see my own herbs growing on our own land."

Harry smiled ruefully. Sukey had been trained as a herb woman by a little old black lady, a former slave. She had a really green thumb for growing things and liked gardening, but more than that, she fancied treating illnesses. Harry had long since resigned himself to being dosed regularly and often for every sneeze, bruise, and scratch. It would be worse, he suspected, when they were established at Their Place, with no one else to practice on within miles. Ah, well, at least her medicines were never noxious, as were some he could remember from his Army days.

Two more nights they camped along the river's bank and set out the following dawn. And then one morning about ten o'clock, Harry sighted the Olethey. Just at the point where it joined the Allegheny a lone silver maple stood, shimmering in the spring breeze. "There it is," he said—far more calmly than he felt.

They crossed the creek and turned upstream. An hour later they were standing by their very own brook.

It was an anxious, suspenseful moment for Harry. He fussed over the cart, sneaking little peeks at Sukey while she took in Their Place—the brook, the hills around it, the raspberry bushes along the creek.

"Oh, yes, Harry," she exclaimed, turning to throw him a brilliant smile, "it's everything you said and more." She crouched down and took a double handful of earth and leaves. "Ours. Five hundred acres."

In his relief, he laughed aloud.

It was densely overgrown. Last November, when the trees had been bare, you could see dozens of yards in every direction. Now, all was masses of green and deep shade. Only the girdled trees stood leafless, a bleak dead note in the green life all around.

"Come, the dugout is this way."

Harry and Kaspar had girdled trees in two places—one in the flat area along the brook for crop land, the other on higher ground where the cabin would be built. "In springk creek vill be high," Kaspar had warned sagely. "Iss not schmardt to build house vere it can be flooded." The dugout was not far off—they could use it for a root cellar later.

But something had gone wrong. The log walls of the dugout had been knocked down and lay sprawled every which way. The ceiling had fallen in, and the puncheon floor was splintered in places. It looked as if it had been savagely attacked.

Harry stared. "Who—?"

Sukey gave a nervous glance over her shoulder. "Maybe it just—fell down," she said.

"*I* might build something that would just fall down, but do you really think Kaspar would?"

"No, I guess not," she agreed reluctantly. They looked at one another, neither wanting to say the word that was trembling on their lips: "Indians." An Indian was the one thing that Sukey was afraid of.

"It might be wild animals," Harry offered. "They say bears like to claw trees." They looked, but there were no claw marks.

"Or the weather perhaps. Suppose lightning struck it or a bad storm washed away one of the base logs."

All those were possibles, but it was much more likely to have been the hand of man. Especially—Harry remembered with a pang—since there was also a well-trampled path leading right to the salt spring. Land east of the Allegheny and near the Forks had been purchased from the Indians by the Penns and was supposed to be safe for settlement. But not all members of a given tribe agreed with purchase treaties, and suppose they were living near some group determined to keep out the whites?

Well, that risk had always been part of frontier life. They would have to face it.

"No use standing here," Harry said. "I'll have to rebuild."

He pulled out the fallen logs and restacked them as walls, pinning them into place with the uprights that

supported the ceiling. He had to make fresh puncheons to replace the splintered section, but by late afternoon the dugout was fit to move into.

While Sukey arranged their belongings and started supper, Harry took his sickle down to the brookside clearing to slash away undergrowth. He wanted to lose no time getting his crop in.

That night, their scare forgotten, they sat before their own fire on their own land, and Harry had an eerie thought. Were they the first of many Warrilows to occupy this land? Would people—oh, long after Harry himself was gone—point to this spot and say, "That's the old Warrilow place. Been Warrilows there as long as anyone can remember."

"What's the matter, Harry?"

"Eh?"

"You shivered. Are you cold? Shall I make you some pennyroyal tea?"

"Oh, no. Just excitement. Shall I read the deed?"

"Oh, yes, yes. Now it really has meaning."

6

Cabin Raising

Harry started clearing at dawn, Sukey working at his side. By the end of the day, they had removed brush and small trees from a good acre on both sides of the brook. The big trees would remain until next winter, when Harry could burn them off.

The following day they planted corn—Indian fashion, with corn, beans, and squash all in the same mound. The corn would provide a stake up which the beans could twine, and the squash would spread out on the ground between the mounds. Later when the rich forest mold had lost some of its fertility, they would bury a fish in each mound for fertilizer.

His two years with the Wertmüllers had given Harry a healthy respect for Indian corn. It had a dozen uses. When fresh, it could be roasted in the ear and eaten with butter and salt like a vegetable. (The first time it was served to him, Harry had politely tried to eat the cob.) When dried, it could be hulled and ground and used as a grain—for pudding and cake and pone and mush and quick bread. The husks of the ear made excellent mattress stuffing, and the stripped cob could be turned into a smoking pipe or a child's doll, or burned as fuel. The stalk and leaves that were left could then be dried out in shocks and used as animal fodder. Corn had only one drawback: It could not be sown like other grains but had to be planted individually in mounds. But in a stump-filled field, there was no other way to plant anyway.

After corn, they rough-cleared another two acres and put in barley and rye, which Harry would need for his distilling, and then Sukey's herbs and some vegetables. By the end of the second week, all the seeds were in the ground. It would be a small crop but enough for a run of the still and to keep them over winter. Harry felt good and gave himself an afternoon off to go hunting.

After that, Harry sharpened up the felling ax and got at the business of cutting timber for the cabin. He chose trees at least a foot thick and fourteen feet long, felled them, lopped off the tops and lower branches. He then squared them with the broadax and notched the ends (squared-logs sat closer on one another than round ones and made a warmer house). By working hard, he could finish three logs in two days.

And while Harry chopped and hacked, Sukey did the weeding, scoured the woods for berries, and kept watch over their brush-burning fire and the trotline they'd strung across the Olethey. She was nervous about Indians and didn't like to venture far from the clearing or have Harry do so. She said nothing about it, but Harry guessed she was pretty anxious for the cabin to be finished, so they'd have more secure shelter at night.

When the sun was high, the two would meet by the

brookside, dangle their feet in the cold rushing water, and eat whatever Sukey had found and prepared for dinner. They had plenty of fish—bass and trout mostly—and soon there were carrots and beets to pull. After the meal, it was back to work until near sundown, when Harry always knocked off to hunt something for the pot—and sometimes succeeded. After supper, they'd sit hugging their knees in the evening cool, companionable.

Sometimes it didn't seem real to Harry that they could actually be here, on their own land, working for themselves, making a farm out of the forest. It was exhausting labor. Harry went to sleep at night dead weary and aching. And yet it wasn't like plain work. You did that mechanically and then collected your pay and your keep in return, and that was that. Working like this to make a farm—well, you won your keep, of course, but you won something more, something that didn't get spent up. You had your farm, and it was yours in a way that a farm you bought—supposing you were rich and could just buy a farm—could never be.

Their deed was important, but that was for other people. What made the farm truly theirs was their labor.

It was full summer by then and hot, but they had to keep a fire going in front of the dugout all night, for there were wolves in the area. They could hear them at twilight, calling assembly: *Ah-ooooooooooo!* A chilling sound, much more blood curdling than the cougar's scream, which they heard after dark.

One night Sukey shook Harry awake. "Look," she whispered.

Three wolves sat in a row on the other side of the fire, staring with their yellow-gray eyes at the two human fig-

ures. Harry reached for his rifle, but with his finger on
the trigger, he couldn't bring himself to pull. Instead,
he lowered it and said, "Shoo. Go away."

"Harry!"

"Scat!"

A moment more, then the great gray-brown beasts rose
and padded silently off.

"Why didn't you shoot? There's a bounty on them in
Pittsburgh."

"I know, but—" He pondered his own actions. "It was
their staring that way, I reckon. So direct and calm. You
can't shoot something that looks you in the eye, any more
than you can shoot someone you've been introduced to."

"Harry, Harry, sometimes I wonder about you."

With the logs for the house all cut and squared,
including the short ones that would form the gable end,
Harry set to with froe and maul to split out shakes for the

roof and puncheons for the floor. "The material is about assembled," he said to his sister one hot night in August. "We'll soon have to look for a crew to roll up the walls."

"Isn't Pittsburgh the only likely place? At least we know people there."

He glanced at her sharply. "MacBain?"

"Yes, and the Semples and the Richards. The tavern people wouldn't come themselves, but they'd know of others."

Meaning that MacBain *would* come himself—and probably bring a crew as well. And put them under yet more obligation. And get in some more licks courting Sukey.

"The potatoes are ready to be dug," Sukey went on. "Take some along to sell and with the money buy kegs. You'll need them for the whiskey, come fall."

"Potatoes won't pay for laboring wages."

She looked at him, troubled. "Do you really think we'll have to pay? Cabin raisings are things everybody pitches in for."

"If people were our neighbors, we could ask, Sukey. But we're forty miles from Pittsburgh and have no close ties there. We don't even have enough fixings to throw them a feast."

There was a marked pause. Then Sukey said, "Mr. MacBain would come. I'm certain of that." She went pink.

Harry mumbled something about Pittsburgh not being able to spare the smith for the length of time it would take. He was ashamed of himself, putting his silly jealousy ahead of her terror and need for shelter. But he did it just the same.

He put off thinking about the problem of cabin raising. He had a good excuse just then, for their crops were ripening. They had roasting ears for dinner every day and were kept busy pulling potatoes and other root vegetables and picking the beans that hung, long and green, from their cornstalk supports. Harry also spent part of each day on another project: beavering down a gigantic, four-foot-thick beech that he had found halfway up one of their hills. It took days to saw and hack the trunk into three pieces and roll them down to the clearing, where with fire and knife and patience he hollowed out three barrels. He would need them for mash when it came time to distill. That done, he stalled some more by hollowing out three buckets from smaller trees. They would do for kegs.

It was well into September by then and the cabin not up. He was standing in front of one of his cut timbers one morning, wondering what to do, when Sukey came to him. "Harry, there's no help for it," she said in her firmest voice. "You'll have to go to Pittsburgh. We must have a cabin before frost sets in."

He was slowly coming to that conclusion himself and yet he resisted: "If only we had rope. We could use a tree limb as a pulley and haul the timbers up the way sailors haul cargo."

"Buy rope in Pittsburgh then."

"Buy? With what?"

"I've been thinking about that, and you know, Harry, we have something much more valuable than anything we could grow."

"What?"

"Why, salt."

He stared at her, astonished. "Of course! Why didn't *I* think that!" Salt brought twenty shillings a bushel. A poke of it would be enough to hire a man for two days, easily.

"I suppose it will take a while to boil out enough," Sukey

went on, "especially since we can only spare one kettle. But if we start right in—"

"We don't have to boil it out. There's plenty on the rocks."

They took the bake kettle and set off immediately for the salt spring, which was in a little fold of the hills above the dugout. The ground was contoured in such fashion that the spring's overflow did not join the brook or even the Olethey but trickled over rocks in the general direction of the Allegheny. All along its edges were encrustations of white and gray, which flecked off easily under Harry's knife. Two hours work, and the bake kettle was nearly full.

Harry surveyed their booty with delight. "Hang it, I'll go tomorrow! In a week we'll have the cabin—"

He broke off. A shout had rung through the woods.

Sukey pressed a hand to her mouth, her eyes wide with alarm. They had gone so long unmolested that Harry had ceased to carry the rifle wherever he went, and it was back at the dugout now. "Let's get home," he said, low.

"Oh, Harry, do you think it's—you know?"

"Oh, it wouldn't be Indians," he said with more confidence than he felt. "Not that noisy."

Just then there was another shout, and this time he could make out the words: "Harry! Miss Susannah! Y'all here?"

Harry and Sukey looked at one another. *MacBain!* Even as he saw relief come over his sister's face, Harry found exasperation replacing fear in his own insides. All the trouble he'd taken not to go to Pittsburgh and ask MacBain for help, and now this!

"What can he be doing here?" Sukey wondered aloud as they pressed forward.

They found the smith in the middle of their stumpy cornfield, scratching his black head. At sight of them, his face lighted up, and he doffed his hat and bowed.

"Mornin', Miss Susannah. Mornin', Harry. We were startin' to think y'all were lyin' somewhere scalped."

Sukey didn't seem to know what to say. "But why are you—what are you doing—?"

"Wal, now, I figgered maybe y'all might be 'bout ready for a cabin raisin', and seein's there ain't nobody much up thisaways, I brought me a couple boys to lend us a hand." He nodded toward two strangers lounging under a tree.

"Why . . . that's very thoughtful, Mr. MacBain. We were in some difficulty over that, it's true. Weren't we, Harry?"

"Yes," said Harry, unable to keep the curtness out of his voice, "but we'd just solved it."

"We haven't much to offer you by way of a feast. Fish, some garden truck, that's all."

"Why, you just put out the rest of Harry's jug, ma'am, and that there'll be plenty feast for us. Right, boys? This here's Tom Reid, and this bald old coot is Sandy Gillespie."

They set to without delay. The timbers were lying scattered about the woods, where the trees had been felled, and the first thing to do was collect them. With MacBain holding one end of a timber and Harry the other, they positioned the first log where Sukey said she wanted the cabin to stand. That marked the back of the house. Reid and Gillespie laid their first log where the front would go. Then they notched in the first side logs and laid the puncheon floor, pinning the ends to the foundation logs with nails—whole handfuls of which MacBain had brought with him.

The walls went up rapidly after that, the men nipping from Harry's jug as they worked. "Harry, you cut these timbers right good," MacBain said at one point. "Notches fit ever' time."

In spite of himself, Harry warmed. He had taken pains to measure with care, and it was pleasant to have a skilled workman like MacBain acknowledge it. Besides, you can't sulk when you're working hard. It oozes out of you along with the sweat.

When the walls were five logs high all around, they stopped to cut an opening in one of the sides where the fireplace would be. Two more logs around, and they quit for the day.

In spite of Sukey's protestations, it was quite a respectable feed that she put out for them: broiled trout, beans, corn on the cob, cornpone, and pennyroyal tea all around. "It's strengthening," she insisted, and Harry smiled to himself to see MacBain meekly drink. The smith had managed to maneuver himself a seat beside Sukey, and gradually their voices grew lower and lower, their conversation more and more private.

Reid and Gillespie—Harry suspected they'd been asked to keep him distracted—launched into the latest gossip. The governor of Virginia—a "gen-yew-ine" earl—had paid Pittsburgh a visit that last summer. Town was comin' up in the world, for a fact. Then, too, they'd heard that the great tea boycott, which had been in effect off and on since 1767, was about to be broken.

"Yessir," Reid said, wagging his head, "this here fella, come from t'other side the mountains, he says the gov'ment in London's sendin' over a parcel of ships with tea so all-fired cheap that ain't nobody not goin' to buy it."

"That should put Boston's nose out of joint," Harry said sourly. He had spent many unhappy months in the Massachusetts capital during his Army days.

"Ain't only Boston, this fella says. Philadelphy's riled up, too, and same for Charleston."

"Lot of fuss over nothing, it strikes me."

"No, it ain't. It's them people in London puttin' taxes on us and tellin' us what all we can do and what all we can't. You got a right nice piece of propitty here. How'd you like it iffen some big old lord in London decided to put a tax on it?"

Harry stared. "Why should they want to do that?"

"No tellin'. But iffen we give in on the tea tax, no sayin' what they could put on us next."

It was difficult to imagine the long arm of King George reaching into the Allegheny Valley to tax Harry. He had his Penn deed, didn't he? His all-important piece of paper? Still, the thought disturbed him some, even caused him not to notice immediately that Sukey and MacBain had gone for a stroll in the twilight.

The first thing they did the following day was cut the doorway and beside it a small window. Then two more logs all around. With the walls this high, even two men couldn't lift the heavy timbers, so they cut saplings, leaned them against the walls like shoring, and slid the timbers up them into place. Even so, it took three men to manage the upper logs. While Reid, MacBain, and Harry went on with the wall raising, Sandy Gillespie, who was a carpenter by trade, hunted out a suitable oak, felled it, and sawed out two-inch-thick planks for the door and window shutter and thinner pieces to shape doorways and window frame.

By afternoon, they were ready to lay the garret floor, which was of puncheon like the cabin floor. The rounded sides facing downward would be their ceiling. The gable ends went up next, the ends evened off with the saw to make a snug fit. Horizontal crosspieces tied the two gables together, and the shakes were laid over them.

By suppertime it actually looked like a house.

The third day was for finishing touches. Gillespie hung the door, using the hinges and latch that MacBain had made. He had to improvise hinges of leather for the shutter. Both were provided with stout bars. He also bored a series of holes up the wall beside the door and drove stout pegs into them. That would be their ladder to the loft.

The other three spread out through the woods, collecting sapling-sized timbers, and notching them for the fireplace and chimney. It rose with great speed. Then with damp clay from the brook bed and some mud, they gave it a fireproof lining. Harry had promised himself that there would be a stone fireplace some day soon and had already begun collecting rocks for it, and now he insisted that at least the hearth should be stone from the beginning. As a dramatic touch, MacBain mounted his swinging crane.

Then the four men stood back and surveyed their handiwork, pleased with themselves. "There, now, Miss Susannah, they's your house for you," MacBain announced grandly. "Jest itchin' to have your pretty foot cross the doorstep."

"It's not quite finished yet," Sukey said. She went down to the brookside, where all summer long she had been nursing a lilac cutting brought from the East. She dug it up and planted it carefully beside the door. "There!" she said, dusting her hands.

On the whole, Harry's sister was strictly practical, but she had her standards, and a house plain wasn't a house if it didn't have a lilac bush by the kitchen door.

So they were roofed and housed at last, and not a moment too soon, for two days after MacBain and his friends said good-bye and departed by boat for the Forks, they saw their first Indian.

7

Showanyaw

Harry was busy picking the last of the corn and beans and shocking the stalks, while Sukey dried out some of her precious herbs and slices of pumpkin over the fire. The wild grapes were just coming ripe, and the woods smelled grapey and rich. Harry had just drawn in a deep breath of the delicious scent when Sukey's startled "Aah!" rang across the clearing.

He turned. A young hunter stood at the edge of the woods, scalplocked and naked except for breechclout, moccasins, and bead necklace.

"Go away!" Sukey shouted at him and then ran toward the cabin. "Harry, make him go away."

After the initial shock, Harry's heart had settled down to a steady, rapid drumming. He took his rifle and walked across the clearing to put himself between his sister and the Indian. "What do you want?" he demanded.

The newcomer said something in his own language.

"I don't understand." They were about ten feet apart by then. The Indian gazed at him quite directly, rather like the wolves that night in summer. He wore no warpaint, Harry noted. Again, he said something in his own language.

"Harry," Sukey called from the cabin door, "make him go away."

"I don't think he's hostile," he called back.

"Hostile or not, *make him go away!*"

The Indian paid no attention to Sukey. He again said something to Harry, then pointed to his right arm. Harry glanced at it, puzzled. A moment more, then the Indian picked up a twig from the ground and snapped it, and again pointed to his arm.

"He's injured!" Harry cried. "He has a broken arm."

He went forward. Yes, now that he looked closer, he could see that the forearm was swollen and misshapen. "Come out into the light," he said, gesturing, and the Indian followed him without objection. But he had barely had time to look at the arm before Sukey brushed him aside. Doctoring was her department. Seen in the light of a patient, the newcomer was anything but unwelcome.

"It will have to be set," she said. She looked at the young man and made a grimace, then pointed to the break.

He nodded, slowly and uncertainly.

"I'll need your help, Harry."

"Have you ever set a bone before?"

"No, but I've seen it done. Here, you hold the upper arm. Firm now."

"All right." Harry took a tight grip, fingers closing around luxuriant muscles. Inwardly he marveled that the injured man trusted them so implicitly. He didn't think, if positions were reversed, that he would trust himself to an

Indian. Or would he? If he were alone in the woods, say, and unable to help himself?

Sukey took the man's hand in her own right. "This is going to hurt, I'm afraid," she said.

He replied in his own language, but the tone indicated that he understood.

"Now don't relax your grip, Harry." Slowly she pulled on the forearm, left fingers exploring the swollen part. The patient's face got a bit puffy, but he didn't make a sound. "Both bones are broken," Sukey reported. "There, that's got one. I know I'm hurting him, but I have to take my— Ah, there's ... the other. Right." Slowly she released the arm, fingers guiding the bones back into place. "Good."

The patient stared at her stonily for a moment, then his face relaxed and he grinned at her, engagingly. She smiled back and patted his cheek.

"We'll need something for a splint," she said briskly. "Bark will do, I think. Harry, please cut me a piece—about so long. Elm bark is probably best."

She took the patient up to the cabin while Harry hunted for an elm and carved out a square foot of bark. By the time he returned, Sukey had made some herb tea and was urging it on the patient. She took the bark, lined it with corn husks for softness, and bound it around the injured limb with strips torn from her shift. Another strip made a sling to tie around his neck.

"There! Now if you just drink your tea like a good— Here, where are you going?"

For the Indian, his arm patched up, was preparing to leave. He nodded to them gravely in turn, then headed for the door. Sukey got there first. "No, no! You should stay until that knits properly!" she insisted. "Harry, make him stay."

"A few minutes ago, it was 'Harry make him go away,' " he said, grinning.

"Oh, Harry, don't be silly. We can't let him go off until it heals. He might jar it loose again—the bone might pierce the skin, and then he'd lose the arm."

"I think he thinks we're keeping him prisoner," Harry said dubiously.

He pointed at the Indian with the unmistakable "you" gesture, put his hands together and laid his head on them in pantomime of sleeping, and then pointed to the ground. The Indian watched him warily while Harry tried to think of a gesture that would say "until your arm heals." In the end he just indicated the arm and repeated his you-stay-here motions. The man seemed to understand. At least he made no further move to leave and even accepted and drank Sukey's tea.

Setting down the cup, he drew a pipe and tobacco from a pouch hanging at his belt and lighted it with a firebrand. Solemnly he blew a breath of smoke north, south, east, and west, then handed the pipe to Harry. Harry had never smoked before and nearly choked on his first puff, but he managed to imitate the Indian's actions in clumsy fashion. That done, their guest touched himself on the breast. "Showanyaw," he said.

Harry pointed to himself and said, "Harry Warrilow," pointed to his sister and said, "Sukey Warrilow."

"Harrywarrilow," he repeated, and thereafter that was how he addressed Harry.

Showanyaw stayed for the rest of September and all of October. They gave him Sukey's plank bed on the lower floor, and Sukey joined Harry in the loft. He was an inch or two shorter than Harry and very slender, feather-light on his feet. His earlobes had been cut so that the rim was attached only top and bottom, and feathers and beads were strung to the dangling part. He laughed and smiled a lot and chattered away in his own tongue, not caring that he was not understood. Harry soon fell into the same habit, for sound is more comfortable than silence.

The first day, when he saw Harry take down his rifle, powder horn, and bullet pouch, he promptly joined the hunting expedition. Harry wasn't especially happy about that at first, knowing he was going to look pretty bad to someone who was certain to be a first-rate hunter himself. But in the end he was glad of Showanyaw's company, because he started right in to teach him a thing or two.

Harry would have strolled off in any direction, but Showanyaw stopped him, tested the wind with a wet finger, and then indicated that they should head in the direction from which the wind was blowing. A few minutes' steady walking through the woods, and they came to a turkey tree—half a dozen or so of the great birds roosting in its branches. Harry gazed at his companion in astonishment. He had hardly seen a single turkey all summer, and now this.

But when he raised his rifle and fired, he missed. Showanyaw shook his head in wonder and said something in his own tongue. Harry shrugged. "I'm a rotten shot," he said frankly.

The birds had all fluttered up at the sound of the shot, gobbling and squawking. After a minute, they all settled down again in the same tree. Harry reloaded and raised his rifle, but Showanyaw stopped him from pulling the trigger until he himself had gone behind Harry and sighted down the barrel. He directed a slight adjustment in Harry's aim and then tapped him on the shoulder in a go-ahead gesture. Harry fired, and one of the birds fell dead.

"Partner!" Harry cried, delighted, as they went to pick up their prey.

From then on they went hunting together nearly every day, and Showanyaw took charge of aiming. On their third such enterprise, they shot a quail—Harry's first. They had so much meat while he was with them that keeping it became a problem. Salt was readily available of course, but barrels and kegs were not, so they ended up drying it over a fire, Indian fashion.

Harry had not had a crony since his Army days, but now, even though they could not speak to one another, he and Showanyaw became mates. Working as well as he could with his one hand, the Indian made Harry a bow and three arrows and directed him to practice with that, thus polishing up his aim without wasting powder and shot. He could contrive to pull the bowstring himself awkwardly, so every evening they had target practice.

One afternoon, when he had been with the Warrilows three days, Showanyaw led Harry some distance down the Allegheny to a secluded cove. There, he pulled aside some undergrowth and revealed a canoe. Evidently he had hidden it here when he first went to get help. It was a beautiful little vessel—a real birch-bark like those made by the Great Lakes Indians. They were rare in the Ohio Valley and brought high prices in trade. Thereafter, they took their hunting expeditions by water.

Another day, Showanyaw set about building a mysterious little structure of saplings held together by strips of grapevine, a miniature wigwam. Harry went to help him with it, and at his instructions cut swatches of bark to cover the framework. When it was finished, Showanyaw brought stones that he had been heating in an outdoor fire and a bucket of water. He urged Harry to join him in the little hut, and out of curiosity Harry did.

Inside, Showanyaw stripped naked, and in a what-the-heck mood, Harry followed suit. Then the water was dumped on the hot stones, sending up clouds of steam, which enveloped the pair with its damp, healing heat. Harry rubbed his bare arms, enjoying the feel of sweat gathering on his skin. Soon he was dripping.

Showanyaw began to speak but not as though to Harry. A ritual of some kind? Harry wondered. He didn't care. The steam felt marvelous. He emerged at the end of an hour, cleansed and refreshed.

Sukey wasn't very pleased with all this romping. Harry still did his work, chinking the cabin, husking corn and scraping the kernels from the cobs, sickling and threshing the barley and rye. But with Showanyaw lounging about, it was easy to find a pretext for quitting early.

"Harry, he's teaching you bad habits," Sukey warned him one day.

"He's teaching me some good ones, too."

"Do you want to become just another shiftless back-woodsman? Like that Girty creature?"

"I won't turn woodsy, Sukey. Showanyaw knows a lot of skills that will be useful."

"And what about your distilling? You ought to get at that."

Harry drew in a long breath and expelled a gusty sigh. He'd been worried about that himself. It was all those lurid tales people told of Indians and liquor—how it drove some of them plain crazy, sent them into a yelling, brawling frenzy. Showanyaw might not be like that, but Harry didn't want to take a chance on it.

"I reckon I'll wait till after he's gone."

"You mean because—? Oh, but Showanyaw isn't *that* kind of Indian!"

"How do we know? Have we seen him in liquor?"

"No, but he's—well, the easygoing sort, good natured."

"A light heart, I grant you." Harry grinned ruefully. Only that morning Showanyaw had been mimicking Harry's heavy tread with an exaggerated stamp-stamp-stamp motion. "But liquor so often changes a man's—well, his nature."

"You're afraid of seeing him drunk, aren't you?"

"Yes, I am. Aren't you?"

"No," she said stoutly. "I simply don't believe he's the sort. Besides, I'm afraid that if you put it off too long, the brook will be frozen over."

That had troubled Harry, too, for he needed flowing water to cool the condenser coils. It was full autumn by now, the woods golden and scarlet on all sides, and already there had been several nippy nights. "Well," he said reluctantly, "I can get started at least—malt the barley."

Showanyaw watched with puzzled eyes as Harry dampened barley in his homemade barrel and then lugged it up to the loft of the house and spread it out to sprout. "I reckon it looks daft,"Harry explained as though he could understand, "but this is the only warm place I have." It was pleasant to be the expert for once.

Showanyaw took a sharp interest in the proceedings once the smell of the mash told him that Harry was making whiskey. He peered, fascinated, at the still beer collecting on top of the fermenting mash and even tasted it.

Once started, the still had to be kept running without letup, and they finished the final distilling by the light of pine knots long after dark. Harry flung himself down at the supper table, dead exhausted and jubilant. They had three full kegs of whiskey and some over in a birch-bark tray that Showanyaw had hastily made when it began to look as if they'd need it.

But his joy was short-lived. For Showanyaw followed him in, carrying the tray, and indicated by gesture that he wanted to drink the contents. Heart sinking, Harry looked at him and then at Sukey. The dilemma was severe.

In a sense he owed the whiskey to his friend—they would not even have been able to save this last bit except for Showanyaw's quick thinking. And he had helped with the work, too. But Harry simply could not bear the thought of seeing him drunk.

"No," he said. "Not for you." He took the tray and put it on a shelf.

A black look came over Showanyaw's face. He pointed to the clearing outside and spoke angrily, tapping himself on the breast.

"No," Harry said and shook his head.

The Indian turned to Sukey and railed at her until she shrank back behind Harry.

"Showanyaw, if I thought you'd drink just a little, I'd be glad to let you have it," Harry said earnestly, trying his best to put the sense of what he was saying into his tone. "But men say that Indians lose all control when they drink and don't stop until the last drop is gone."

But this produced only a further torrent of angry words, and Harry had to fall back on shaking his head. "No," he said, "no, no, no."

Black eyes blazing, Showanyaw glared at Harry. Then with a single, savage motion, he tore the bark splint off his arm, flung it at their feet, and tore out of the cabin into the night.

8
Disputed Territory

Harry missed Showanyaw badly and regretted that they had parted in bad blood. But Sukey was almost relieved. "The arm must be pretty well healed by now," she pointed out, "and he would have left soon anyway."

"All the same, I feel as if I've cheated him in some fashion. I should have waited before distilling. I shouldn't have tempted him."

"Oh, Harry, you and your fancies!"

"If only I could have explained."

"Well, you couldn't, and there's no sense worrying about it."

"No, I reckon not."

For a few days, Harry kept hoping that Showanyaw would get over his anger and come back. Then gradually he got used to the fact that he was gone for good.

They began to talk about what they would buy with their kegs. A really large kettle—they were agreed on that.

They would need it next spring for sugaring off, and in the meantime it would serve for salt boiling and Sukey's soap making. But what else? Powder and lead, of course. Some flaxseed. Sukey wanted Harry to hire some men to help fell trees and clear more land, so they could sow pasture grass and bring in sheep for wool and maybe a yoke of oxen. Harry wanted a brood sow; pigs didn't need pasture and could survive nicely in the woods, and that way they'd be assured a meat supply.

"Well, I reckon I'd best wait and see what they say in Pittsburgh." He glanced at her shyly. "You want to come with me?"

"You don't think I can survive by myself a few days?"

"No, but I reckoned you might like to see a bit of company."

"I'm quite happy here, thank you."

That was a relief. Why couldn't he get up the nerve to ask her straight out how she felt about Anse MacBain? Was he afraid what the answer would be?

The kegs were far too heavy for Harry to cart, so all he could do was wait until the river froze and then haul his whiskey by sledge. Throughout November, Harry and Sukey watched the weather anxiously. The first snow came and quickly melted. Then ice began to form around the edges of the rocks in the brook, and the rain turned to sleet and then more snow. The creek was soon down to a narrow run of water between two sheets of ice.

By December the Allegheny was nearly closed over. "Shall we risk it?" Harry asked his sister.

"No, not yet, Harry. Wait till January. Give the ice time to freeze solid."

Impatient to go—for it was their first crop, their first

proof that they could survive and prosper in the woods—Harry spent the time boiling salt and clearing land. There were stumps and fallen trees everywhere. When he came back from Pittsburgh, he would have a burning off.

For weeks after Showanyaw left, he had not had the heart to go hunting, but now the urge came back. Tracking was easy in the snow. He found deer marks everywhere, and by following them patiently he would sooner or later catch up. He killed three the first week. There was no difficulty about keeping the meat in this cold weather, and Sukey needed the hides to make moccasins and shoepacks.

By Christmas the snow was three layers deep and crusty on top. If Harry was going to travel forty miles afoot, he would need snowshoes. He wasn't certain how they were made, but at least he had learned from Showanyaw how to bend wood. He consulted Sukey about what wood to choose, and she said ash or hickory, so he collected some thin limbs of each and experimented. He peeled them and then heated them over the cabin fire, as Showanyaw had showed him. Ash seemed somewhat more pliable, so he settled for that.

When the frame had been properly bent and lashed, he made holes for the laces by burning with a nail. He had started to thread strips of deerhide into the holes when Sukey stopped him. "They need cross pieces, Harry, to stiffen the frame. Also they ought to turn up a bit at the tip."

He corrected for this and then began lacing haphazardly back and forth. When he was done, he had a pretty messy looking pair of snowshoes, but they would serve.

Sukey had been watching him work in silence. Now she spoke up abruptly: "Make a second pair, please, Harry."

"Eh?"

"I've changed my mind. I'm coming with you."

By the middle of January, Sukey thought the ice on the Allegheny looked solid enough. So they set out at dawn through a stinging wind, Harry drawing a crude sledge that he had improvised out of shakes and pegs. It was loaded with the kegs of whiskey, little bags of Sukey's dried herbs, and two bark containers of salt.

Harry stopped at the edge of the clearing to look back at the little cabin huddled under its roof of snow. "I'll be glad to get home," he said and shot an apprehensive glance at his sister. "Won't you?"

"Of course I will! But come along now. We have a great distance to travel."

Harry had been practicing with his snowshoes and no longer stepped on himself when turning around, so the going was fairly easy. The Allegheny was a tumbled, jumbled mass of blue-white ice, where it had been cracked and thrown up and then frozen again. They often had to travel far out in the middle or cross from one side to the other and back again, to avoid these pile-ups. Still, the river was an open highway that would eventually take them where they were going—if they didn't freeze first.

The weather was bitter indeed. They both wore moccasins inside shoepacks, with cornhusk for insulation, but as on their mountain journey, they had to stop two or three times a day and light a fire to get the circulation going again in numb toes.

They made much better time than they had with the handcart through the woods. They spent the night in a brush shelter, huddling under their worn old bearskin. Then it was up at dawn again and on to Pittsburgh. It was just early winter dusk when the orchard of the public garden came into view.

"We'll go to Semple's," Sukey insisted. "Mrs. Semple will be glad to put us up for a poke of salt." It was her way of saying, We're not penniless scrimpers and makeshifters now. We're property owners with a valuable crop to sell.

As they came down the Forbes road, to where it met the Braddock, they noticed that the gates of Fort Pitt were closed and that a businesslike soldier stood sentry in front of it. "That's odd," Sukey said.

But Harry hardly heard. He had been worrying about MacBain every frozen step of their journey, and now as they neared the village, his fears increased by leaps and bounds. He knew he was being ridiculous, but this did not stop his stomach from trembling. As they turned up the Braddock road, he was feverishly trying to think how to avoid passing the smithy.

But Sukey calmly turned into Ferry Street and headed straight for Ferry and Water, and he could only follow. Suddenly she stopped. "Harry, doesn't it strike you that there are an awful lot of armed men in town?"

"Eh?"

"Look, there and there. And that tavern is simply bursting."

He was about to answer something vague about all frontier people going armed when a casual glance around told him that she was right. It was like a town with an occupying army, except that they wore no uniforms. "And the sentry at Fort Pitt! Something must be going on."

"We can stop and ask Mr. MacBain," Sukey said, and Harry's heart lurched sickeningly.

A; it turned out, however, the yard of the smithy was so crowded with men and horses that they could not get near enough to speak to the smith. Harry was almost limp with relief as they passed on to Semple's.

But a few minutes later, relief changed to consternation, for Mrs. Semple told them the news.

Sukey had just made her bargain with the landlady, and as the salt was being measured out, she asked casually who all the men in town were. "Virginians," said Mrs. Semple brightly. "They came with John."

"John?"

"My son-in-law, Captain Connolly. We're to be part of Virginia now."

For a moment Harry simply did not understand what she meant. Happily she explained. "John" had been chosen by his dear good friend Lord Dunmore, Royal Governor of Virginia, to come to Pittsburgh and set up the county of West Augusta under Virginia's control. He had posted a proclamation to that effect and called a muster of militia for the twenty-fifth of the month.

"But this is Pennsylvania!"

"We believe," she said primly, "that Pennsylvania's western border lies along Laurel Ridge. See, there's a copy of the proclamation now." She nodded toward a paper tacked up over the bar. Harry crossed over and read it numbly.

> Whereas his Excellency, John, Earl of Dunmore . . . [Harry's eye slipped down to the heart of the matter] The necessity of erecting a new County, to include Pittsburgh . . . I hereby require and command all Persons in the Dependency of Pittsburgh to

assembly themselves there as a Militia on the 25th Instant at which time . . .

Sukey joined him, wanting to know what it said. But after he'd told her, she pooh-poohed it. "All this politics, it's nothing to us."

"Nothing, eh? If this is Virginia, what happens to our Penn deed?"

Her eyes widened. "Oh, they couldn't take— But it's legal! Bought and paid for!"

He shook his head grimly. "It's legal only if it's Pennsylvania. How can the Penns sell what isn't theirs?"

"But—what can we do?"

At that moment, the empty barroom suddenly filled up with a dozen or so Virginians, surging in, stamping the snow from their feet, blowing on their hands, and pounding on the bar for service. Harry took his sister by the arm and drew her upstairs to the loft corner where they were to sleep. The action gave him a few seconds to think.

"See here, there must be some Pennsylvanian authorities hereabouts. It strikes me we ought to consult someone who knows his way about."

"Authorities? What authorities? I don't remember any officials last spring."

"That's because we're in Pittsburgh. The county seat is Hannastown."

"Oh, I'd forgotten. Does that mean we have to go to Hannastown?"

Harry snapped his fingers as a brief memory nudged him. "There *is* a judge in town. Remember the man who performed the marriage? Judge MacSomething."

"Good, Harry."

"Mac, Mac, Mac—MacKay, that's it!"

"Go now. Quickly. Supper won't be ready for another half hour."

He plunged down the stairs, paused briefly to ask directions to Judge MacKay's house, and then hurried out into the snowy dusk. The judge lived in a two-story log house which, for Pittsburgh, was an imposing affair. A redheaded serving girl let Harry in and took him to a rather cramped study, where a man sat writing by the combined light of a candle and a roaring fire. He was in his thirties and dressed like a gentleman.

"Yes?" he said.

"Sir, it's about these men here—these Virginians."

The judge sighed. "Yes?"

"Can they really do it, sir? Make this part of Virginia? I mean, I was told all this was Penn land. We bought from Governor Penn himself. I have the deed right here."

The judge put down his pen and looked at Harry for a minute. "We don't know if they can really do it, son."

"But—but *someone* must know."

"The problem, you see, is the original charter," Judge MacKay explained. "The Penns' charter. It says that Pennsylvania is to extend five degrees of longitude west of a certain point on the Delaware. And no one is quite sure where that line lies."

"But hasn't it been surveyed, sir?"

"No. Mr. Mason and Mr. Dixon had intended to run their line the entire distance, but the surveying party was stopped by the Indians. We maintain that the line lies somewhere west of Pittsburgh. Virginia says it's in the mountains."

"You mean she just up and decided that?"

"Well," said the judge, scratching his chin, "her guess is as good as ours, after all. And Virginia fought for the region at a time when Pennsylvanians did not. Built the first little fort—Fort Prince George—right where Fort Pitt now stands."

Yes, it was a Virginian who had started the French war—that guffin of a militia officer.

"The real difficulty," the judge went on, "is that Virginia has a law saying that all able-bodied men must serve in the militia, and Pennsylvania does not. Consequently, Virginia officials are able to show force. So we are obliged for a time to submit."

"Then my land is in danger, sir?"

"Oh, I shouldn't think that. They're bound to respect an

honest mistake in ownership. They may make you pay for it all over again, however. But Virginia sells land for barely half what the Penns ask—one reason they have so many followers."

There was some comfort in that, though not much. "How will the dispute be settled, sir?"

"Well, word has been sent to an official named St. Clair—he lives in Ligonier—and he'll be in touch with Governor Penn. Doubtless Penn will protest to Dunmore, but in the end the decision will probably be made in London."

"London?" Harry said balefully. "What does London know about Pittsburgh?"

"Very little, and that's fact. But since two colonies are involved, the Colonial Office will have to decide between them. Although in the present state of affairs, it wouldn't surprise me," he added, "if the government were pleased to hear of the quarrel. They might even work to keep it going—anything to prevent the colonies from uniting."

Harry thanked the judge and returned to Semple's, brooding. All their hard-earned money, all the back-breaking labor they had invested, and now some far-off milord somewhere could pick up a pen and with a few strokes take it all away again.

Just when he and Sukey had begun to feel successful, competent to control their destiny, this thunderclap, this reminder that powerful outsiders could do them down whenever they felt like it.

When he reported this conversation to Sukey, however, she took it as, by and large, good news. "We won't worry about losing the farm until it happens," she said. "Come on, supper is just being served."

The center of attention, as they entered the barroom
where the big table was spread, was a rather ordinary-
looking man of middle height, about thirty. The men
swarming around him were all Virginians, and it was
"Whatever you say, Captain . . . fetch a chair for the
captain . . . now don't y'all talk smart to the captain. . . ."
Harry gathered that this was "John." Connolly plainly enjoyed being deferred to, and when Mrs. Semple indicated
that he should take the head chair, he did so with an
air of it's-only-my-due.

The conversation was all about taking up land and
rumors that the Shawnee were on the warpath again.
Then a latecomer took his seat at the table, and since he
was fresh from the East, he was asked for the news.

"Well," said the traveler, "heard 'bout the tea? East India
Company sendin' it over to sell cheap?"

Yes, everyone had heard that.

"Well, damn my eyes iffen it didn't get sent back or
warehoused at ever' last port. And Boston, she up and
dumped the whole cargo in the harbor."

Harry thought, Boston would! But the rest of the table
laughed heartily and hurrahed, and there were shouts
of "Good for Boston!" Even when Captain Connolly
frowned and said austerely that it was a wicked waste of
someone else's money and London was certain to resent it
bitterly, the others continued to express approval. And
for the remainder of the meal, no one talked of anything
but Boston, John Company tea, and what the government
was likely to do about this latest caper.

The meal ended, and the hard-core politics talkers
transferred to stools and cane chairs before the fire.
Harry and Sukey wanted only to get to bed and were
heading up the famous staircase when their names were

called. They looked down, and there, stamping snow from his shoes, was Anse MacBain.

"Miss Susannah, ma'am, your servant," he said, bowing. "I come soon's I heard y'all were in town. But it's Harry I want to talk to."

Harry walked downstairs to meet him, resentment —which for a while had been submerged in his agitation over the news—flooding back. "What is it?"

MacBain jerked his black head to indicate that he wanted to go to a far corner. There, in a low voice, he said, "I don't reckon you and your sister ought rightly to stay all alone up there at that there place of yourn."

"What are you talking about?"

"Injuns, that's what. A risin' is brewin'."

"We haven't been molested." In consternation, Harry suddenly remembered the dugout, all thrown down. He pushed the thought away. "We even had an Indian staying with us for six weeks."

"What! You let your sister live in the same house with a murderin' savage?"

"Showanyaw's *not* a murdering savage!" Harry cried hotly. "We were friends. He taught me lots of things. And, anyway, Sukey is the one who insisted he stay."

MacBain stared heavily. "Rabbit me if I know what to make of you, Harry. A Shawnee, too."

"Shawnee?"

"That's what Showanyaw means."

Harry was startled. He hadn't really given much thought to Showanyaw's tribal affiliations, but he had vaguely considered him a Delaware or one of some other relatively docile and peaceful peoples. The fiery Shawnee now—that was something to think about.

" 'Sides," the smith went on, "that was last year. This year, things is different."

"How?"

"Why, you poor fool, because of Connolly and Dunmore. Lookee here, Pennsylvania's had right good relations with the Injuns most of the time. The savages has respect for the Penns. But they hates Virginians. Now what you think they'll be doin' when they finds out these parts is Virginia?"

9
Maneuvers

In his concern over losing the farm, Harry had not considered what this change in status might mean to the Indians. "But do the Shawnee actually know the difference?" he objected. "I should think all whites would seem alike to them."

"You bet your life they knows the difference. Injuns is plenty smart. You and Miss Susannah had ought to live here awhile, out of their way."

"No, never."

"You think on it."

"No," Harry said strongly. "We have the farm well started. I'm not going to abandon it."

"You think about that sister of yourn. You want to see her all scalped and bloody?"

"Sukey would say the same thing. Believe me, Mr. MacBain—"

"Anse, Anse," the smith put in distractedly.

"I know my sister. She's stubborn about things. We worked and saved a long time to buy that land—and worked even harder this year to clear and plant. It's ours and you don't abandon what's your own. Scared as she is of Indians, Sukey would take the risk."

The smith sighed. "Mebbe I best go to Miss Susannah her own self."

"I wish you wouldn't. You'd just alarm her."

"Lookee here, I ain't sayin' you should give up the place permanent—just move to Pittsburgh till the scare's over."

"The scare might last for months. We couldn't afford to live in Pittsburgh for months."

"Be my guests. Got me a good-sized house, Belle to take care of it. It'd pleasure me a whole heap to have Miss Susannah visitin'."

"Sukey would never agree to that in a million years."

MacBain stared at him for a long, silent moment, his black eyes grim. Finally he said, "Then I'm agoin' with y'all."

"What!"

"I'm agoin' with you, set me up a little forge by your cabin."

"You're not serious."

"Dead serious."

"But—but where would you find customers?"

"Spend the time forging hardware, sell it later." And with Harry gaping at him open mouthed, he went on, "You see, the one kind of white man the Injuns really looks up to is a smith. They needs him as much as white men does—to repair guns iffen nothin' else. Iffen they sees a forge 'side your cabin, you got a chance of bein' left alone."

One half of Harry was saying, No, no, my God, not that!

And the other was wondering how much he could accomplish with a second pair of hands to command —double the cabin size, build a barn, clear land a lot faster.

He pulled himself together. "Look, Mr. MacBain, I know you mean it kindly and all, but it's just crazy. You're all established here, with a house and shop and all, and people rely on you. What would Pittsburgh do without a smith?"

"Till the scare's over, Pittsburgh can get along with my striker."

"Suppose I just said plain no—that I won't let you settle on my land?"

"Then I'd move up there and settle in the next valley."

Harry stared at the self-confident smith, thinking, Why can't I ever win with him? "All this 'Indian scare' business," he burst out hotly, "it's nothing but an excuse to come up to the Olethey to court my sister. Isn't it?"

"No, it ain't. Not but what," he added with a small grin, "I ain't lookin' forward to some powerful strong wooin' oncet I'm there."

Harry abruptly turned on his heel and stalked out.

He reported this conversation to Sukey as he was pulling off his shoepacks and moccasins in the pallet-filled garret. It meant having to mention an Indian rising, but she'd heard tales of that at supper already anyway. When he told her about MacBain's insistence that he was going to come and live near them, she gave a little exclamation.

"What a mad thing to think of!"

Harry was still so angry at the smith's presumption that for once he was heedless. "Not so mad. It gives him a chance to pay court to you."

"Court *me*?" But there was a false note in the surprise.

Sukey knew very well that MacBain had his eye on her.

"He told me last spring, that very first day in Pittsburgh, that he was going to be my brother-in-law some day."

He held his breath, hoping for an angry denial. But all she said was "He takes a great deal for granted, doesn't he?"

"He does that. Well, are we to let him come and live with us?"

She was silent a minute. It was too dark in the garret for Harry to see her face, but he thought her breathing had quickened. At last she said, "Well, with two men on the place, think how much faster we can clear."

So, now they were to have MacBain right in the house with them. And this afternoon, Harry had worried about passing the smithy on their way to Semple's!

Early next morning, they started out to sell their produce. The whiskey went very fast and brought a good price, but what surprised them was the demand for salt. Everyone needed salt and told them they were in the greatest of luck to have a salt spring on their property. Salt fetched so much, in fact, that they rapidly lengthened the list of items they would buy. Harry got his sow in farrow. Sukey bought two blankets, and when they went to MacBain to order a large kettle, they added an auger, a trivet, and two smaller kettles for cooking.

"Harry tell you 'bout me agoin' up there with y'all, Miss Susannah?"

"Yes," she said, a bit cool, "but I really don't understand, Mr. MacBain, why you think Harry and I can't take care of ourselves."

"You ever see a Injun raid, Miss Susannah?"

"No." But she couldn't repress a shiver.

"Well, I have. Back in Staunton where I was borned. I ain't agoin' to let you see things like that, no, ma'am, not iffen I can help it."

She gave a little shrug. "It's all right with me. An extra pair of hands will be useful."

Harry wanted to say, "Well, it's not all right with me!" But he held his tongue, and the matter was settled.

The town was still crowded with Virginia militia, most of them mounted, and all clamoring for MacBain to shoe their horses or repair their rifles. When word went out that the smith was planning to leave Pittsburgh, probably for months, the outcry was tremendous. Captain Connolly himself came bustling into the smithy, at the head of a noisy escort.

"See here, man, you can't abandon your post at a time like this! Indians on the warpath, threatening the settlements. A smith is most urgently needed here."

"Sorry, Captain."

"It is your bounden duty to remain. By the authority of my position, I *order* you not to leave."

"I got my own notions 'bout duty, Captain. 'Sides, Charlie's here." He nodded at his striker.

They wrangled away for half an hour, while MacBain and Charlie calmly went on making the Warrilows' giant kettle—*tink . . . clang . . . tink . . . clang*—until finally Connolly flung off in wrathful defeat. Harry knew how he felt.

Their purchases made, there was nothing for Harry and Sukey to do but lounge about restlessly, waiting for MacBain to finish forging their new equipment. He took his time about it—stalling, Harry suspected, though it's true he did have to stop now and then to shoe some important horse.

Captain Connolly was much in evidence in Pittsburgh, they noticed, striding about through the snow, accompanied by a tough-looking escort and an air of bristly self-importance. He had taken over Fort Pitt, and there was much activity among his followers, one of whom was Simon Girty. As news of Connolly's summoning the militia went out, more and yet more of these hard-faced swaggerers turned up in Pittsburgh. Occasionally one of them would fire wantonly on the Indian encampment across the Allegheny, and little by little it emptied out.

"What is the militia called up for anyway?" Harry asked MacBain.

"To fight Injuns."

"What Indians? Where?"

"Rumors is out, I tell you."

Connolly said the same thing. Harry heard him speechifying one day, all about how they had to gather and go out into the field to protect helpless women and children, how Virginia would shield them from Indian raids while Pennsylvania would not.

"Pennsylvania doesn't have to!" Harry shouted through cupped hands and won a black look for himself. It was a sore point with many Virginians that Pennsylvania had always had much better relations with the tribesmen than they did.

Connolly had opened a land office and was selling acreage as fast as buyers could be found. It was as though he knew the London decision would go against him, and he wanted to skim off as much cream as he could while he could. The price was low by Penn standards, and as Judge MacKay had observed, it won him many followers. Harry was tormented to think how much better equipped they could have been all along if they had bought at Virginia prices. Still, he did not really regret having a Penn deed.

Then one day a newcomer rode into town—from the East. A gentleman he was, broad-faced and commanding in look, and every head turned as he swung off his horse in front of Ormsby's tavern.

"St. Clair," people said, passing the word. "It was St. Clair. Did you see? St. Clair—now we'll see something."

Judge MacKay had mentioned a Mr. St. Clair, Harry remembered. A Pennsylvania official, in touch with the governor. Well, at least they weren't being ignored altogether.

At first, however, St. Clair did nothing. Then on the twenty-fourth, the day before the muster, he acted. Harry, who was lounging before the fire in Semple's barroom, saw the whole thing. Connolly was just crossing the room toward the door when it opened, and the broad-faced man came in. "You are John Connolly?" he said.

"I am."

"You own yourself the author of that paper posted there and elsewhere around town?"

"I do."

"Such a proclamation invites unlawful assembly with an intention to disturb the public peace. As an officer of the county of Westmoreland, I must ask you to supply sureties for your good behavior while resident here."

"The soil we stand on, sir, is Virginia, and you have no authority to act."

"Will you give me sureties or not?"

"I will not."

"Very well, then, you leave me no choice but to take you

to the county jail in Hannastown." He stepped to the door and beckoned, and two stout deputies entered, armed with pistols. "Seize Mr. Connolly and put him on his horse. It is ready saddled at the door."

The three whisked the captain out the door and onto his horse and rode out of town before his turbulent Virginians knew it had happened.

Well, Harry thought, immensely cheered, that's that.

But a week later, still cooling his heels in Pittsburgh, Harry saw Connolly ride jauntily back into town, St. Clair at his heels. "The so-called sheriff saw reason," he explained airily to Mrs. Semple. "I have been released." He smiled complacently, well-pleased with himself.

That night, a wild celebration burst out. The Virginians marched through the streets of the little town, then up the Braddock road to Fort Pitt, where they broached a keg of rum, fired off their rifles, yelled and whooped and generally cut up rough. St. Clair and Judge MacKay hurried off down the road after them and managed to subdue them for a time, but toward nightfall they broke out again. The respectable half of Pittsburgh was kept awake most of the night.

It all seemed ominous to Harry, as though it foretold great upheavals to come. With these frontier ruffians at his beck and call, Connolly could do as he pleased. As it happened, he had been voluntarily released, but there was a good chance that he would have been rescued by his wild followers if the sheriff had not set him free. Judge MacKay might talk lightly of men being bound to respect ownership, but with an army of Simon Girtys floating around, unchecked by responsible authority, it wasn't likely that any kind of property would be safe.

"How much longer will it be?" he demanded of MacBain, anxious to start for home.

"Jest another day, I reckon," said the smith. "Got a heap of things to shift."

They were to travel in style, on horses that the smith had hired, led by professional packtrain‧men. MacBain had to take not only an anvil but a huge bellows and tue iron for his forge and all kinds of tongs, hammers, hardies, and so on, plus coal and raw iron for working. They would be a train of eight horses.

And at last they were ready for the journey. Sukey was to ride pillion behind Harry, their horse a husky beast reputedly strong and surefooted. MacBain rode first in line, then the five pack horses, then Harry and Sukey, and finally the packtrain man. The pig was tied to the pillion on which Sukey rode and trotted along behind. They filed out of town shortly after dawn and started up the ice-filled river.

The horses plodded along, footfalls muted by the snow underfoot. Once in an icy patch, the Warrilows' horse skidded for a moment. But he was wearing winter shoes and quickly got his legs under him again. Harry hadn't ridden a horse since he left the Wertmüllers', so his riding muscles were slack and soon began to complain. Still, his feet swung dry and free.

Actually, they made no greater speed than Harry and

Sukey afoot, because of the snow and the heavy loads. So it was again a two-day journey. Then late in the afternoon of the second day, they rounded a mound of piled-up ice and saw the little silver maple that marked the mouth of the Olethey. They turned up it, Harry more and more eager, and soon they came to the clearing.

Harry half expected to find the clearing devastated, the cabin burned, but there it was, just as they'd left it, looking lonesome. Joyously he dismounted and flung open the door, Sukey a step behind him, admiring the fireplace, the plank bed, the peg ladder to the garret, the log section that served as a chair. He would never love a person—nor would his sister, he thought—as he loved this place.

10
Alarm

The rest of the winter Harry spent clearing timber, cutting down the smaller trees and burning out the big ones. MacBain worked alongside him until he had enough logs for a cabin. He did not bother squaring them, just notched the ends. Then he and Harry rolled up the cabin, setting it well above the original cabin and at right angles to it. Then MacBain set to work finding stone with which to build his forge. By the end of March he was all set up, and they soon grew used to hearing *tink . . . tink . . . tink* all day.

The Allegheny ice had broken up by then. They could hear the great grinding roar of the crashing floes. The spring rains began, and the snow was washed away, and the Olethey rose until it was nearly as wide as the Allegheny. Even the brook was swollen—they had to fell a tree across it as an improvised bridge.

They sugared off just before the last of the snow was gone, collecting the sap in bark vessels and boiling it all day in their big new kettle. Harry loved sugaring off. When the sap got dark and thick, they tossed dollops of it into patches of snow, where it stiffened in odd shapes and became a delicious maply blob.

The pig farrowed. She had spent the winter in a crude lean-to near the outside of the fireplace. Now, however, they turned her loose, and she and her piglets roamed the woods freely, rooting for acorns or anything else edible.

The high water crested and began to recede, and soon it was time to plant. There was plenty of cleared land this year, so Harry put in a big crop, his own seed corn plus more that he had bought in Pittsburgh. Sukey, too, expanded her garden. Of course, the plants still sprouted in the midst of stumps. Harry would get the stumps out eventually—down to plowshare depth, as the Wertmüllers had taught him—but that would have to wait until they had a pair of oxen, and cattle in turn would have to wait until they had a barn and pastureland. The list of things he still did not own stretched ahead of him endlessly.

MacBain slept at the smithy, but he took his meals with the Warrilows. He was unfailingly gallant toward Sukey, solicitous of her opinion, courting away for all he was worth. But Harry had the impression that the courtship had ground to a halt, that the smith had made all the headway he was going to make.

For a time, MacBain's presence had Harry so rattled that he could hardly turn a corner without expecting to surprise them in the act of kissing. He never did, however, and eventually it dawned on him that he had never seen them touching—even casually as in dancing. Was Sukey keeping the smith at arm's length? Harry fervently hoped so.

One day in April the mystery of their thrown-down dugout was solved. They had felt and heard a kind of general rumbling underfoot for nearly an hour—an inexplicable sound, getting closer and closer. They had been asking one another, "What is it? What could do that?" Then up toward the salt spring, they saw the tree branches waving as though disturbed by something, and they all three went up to investigate.

It was a herd of wood bison. Harry gaped. He had never seen anything like these giant beasts with huge shaggy heads and humped backs. Even MacBain, raised on the frontier, had only known about them through hearsay.

They came on in single file, paying no attention to the human onlookers, drank from the salt spring, threw themselves down and rolled in the mud. When they were well caked, they trotted over to the old dugout and scratched themselves. With their horns they hooked out the logs and tossed them down, as though for the pleasure of the experience. Finally they flopped down in the shade.

MacBain got down on one knee and raised his rifle. "We're goin' to have us some beef tonight!" he exulted, taking bead on a large bull.

Harry was just in time to knock the barrel aside. "Not now," he said. He had thought fast. "Look here, if they've returned twice in a row, they probably come here every year. If we turn this place into a slaughterhouse, we'll only drive them away."

"You mean, you're aimin' to let all that meat go?"

"Not entirely. Let's wait until they leave, then pick off the last in line."

Sukey smiled. "Harry's always thinking about next year, the year after, ten years from now."

"No," MacBain said soberly, "this oncet he's right. We wait."

The bison stayed three days. Then they took a final roll in the mud and a final drink from the spring, and fell back into single file. Harry and MacBain shot the last two in line as they trotted off, and there were new buffalo robes for next winter and meat to salt down. The dugout had to be rebuilt, of course, but that seemed a small price.

There seemed to be more people passing through now than last year. Once a long hunter stopped off at the two cabins and brought news from Pittsburgh. Captain Connolly had gone off to Virginia and got himself made a county magistrate. On his return, he created a public scene at the courthouse in Hannastown, arriving for his trial at the head of two hundred armed men and then publicly lecturing the Pennsylvania justices of the peace on the grounds that they had no jurisdiction west of Laurel Ridge. En route back to Pittsburgh, his followers staged a noisy debauch. And at the Forks, he issued warrants for the arrest of Judge MacKay and two others, whom he sent off to Virginia.

Since then, Connolly had been recruiting men, the hard-drinking brawling, noisy riffraff of the frontier, and this crude band did about as it pleased, harassing civilians, seizing supplies, roughing up any Indians who ventured near the town. The countryside was uneasy. Under conditions like these, the Indians could hardly help but go on the warpath.

"No news of a risin' yet?" MacBain inquired.

"Just rumors, same as last winter."

"And what 'bout Boston?"

"Oh, Boston," said the hunter, dismissing the East as of no importance.

A week or two later a trader from Kittanning stayed

overnight with them on his way down to Pittsburgh. He had heard of white-Indian clashes all right, plenty of them, but they were all cases of whites murdering Indians. "It's havin' these here wild Virginians 'round our necks," he complained. "Why, some of them, they can't hardly meet a Injun in the woods 'thout killin' him. It's bad for business. They say the Shawnee and the Mingo is out a'ready and mebbe more to follow."

Their next visitor arrived in the middle of a June night.
Tap, tap, tap . . .
Harry sat bolt upright, heart thumping.
Tap, tap, tap . . .
There! He *had* heard something! He rolled off his pallet, slid across the floor and down the peg ladder. In the blackness, Sukey's face swarmed up from the bed in the corner, a whitish blur. The sound had awakened her, too.
Tap, tap, tap . . . Someone at the door then—prosaically knocking. Except that on the frontier, people didn't make midnight calls unless something was terribly wrong.

Harry lifted down the rifle from its pegs. It was kept loaded, so all he needed to do was cock it. Then he took up his stand beside the bolted door. "Who is it?" he demanded.

"Harrywarrilow! Harrywarrilow!"

Showanyaw! But what on earth—?

"What is it? What do you want at this time of night?"

"Harrywarrilow!" *Tap, tap, tap* . . . "Harrywarrilow!" He added something in his own tongue on an urgent note.

Harry put his hand on the latch. Showanyaw was their friend. Surely he wouldn't— On the other hand, Harry had been warned about Indians by people who were sup-

posed to know them—flighty . . . treacherous . . . change
their minds in a flash. . . .

"Open it, Harry," Sukey said from across the room.

He threw her a troubled look. She'd been too frightened before. Now she was too trusting. As a compromise,
he undid the window shutter and slipped it open an inch.
A shaft of moonlight poked in. "Yes, Showanyaw, what
is—"

He broke off with a heart-stopping gasp. For the
Indian's arm slid into the opening and slammed the
shutter all the way open, and he stood framed in the
bright square like all their nightmares come to life.

For in the brilliant moonlight, they could see that this
was not the simple hunter of last fall. This was a savage on
the warpath. His face and naked upper body were painted
in great patches of red and yellow and black, he wore a
roach of red hairs over his scalp lock, and his earlobes
were strung with feathers and mouse skulls. From the
midst of this barbaric splendor his eyes glittered fiercely
into Harry's as he demanded, *"Poo-sa-va-nee? Poo-sa-va-
nee?"*

For a moment, absolutely numb with terror, Harry had
been unable to move. Then he raised the rifle with one
hand and reached for the shutter with the other.

His finger was closing on the trigger, the muzzle only
inches from the Indian's chest, before Showanyaw appeared to notice it. Then he glanced sharply at Harry's
face as though he couldn't believe his eyes. They stared at
one another a moment longer, frozen. Then Harry slowly
released the trigger and after a moment lowered the
weapon.

"What is it, Showanyaw?" he said, now quite bewildered.
By way of explaining what he had nearly done, he pointed

to the paint and then mimicked the Indian's action in
slamming open the shutter.

Shownayaw brushed all that aside. *"Poo-sa-va-nee?"* he
said for the third time.

It was a question of some kind. "I don't understand,"
Harry said, leaning the rifle against the fireplace. He still
trembled with aftershocks from the fright he'd had, and it
was hard to turn his mind to run-of-the-mill communica-
tions problems.

"Poo-sa-va-nee?" Showanyaw's voice was beginning to
take on an exasperated note. He pointed to Harry and
then to Sukey, who had joined him at the window.
"Poo-sa-va-nee? Poo-sa-va-nee?"

"Poo-sa-va-nee?" Harry echoed.

"Ah." He pointed at Harry. *"Poo-sa-va-nee?"* Then at

Sukey. *"Poo-sa-va-nee?"* When they merely stared back at him, uncomprehending, he turned from the window and fairly danced in the fury of his frustration.

Then Sukey said slowly, "Pennsylvania? Can he possibly—?"

Showanyaw spun around. "Ah, ah, ah! Poo-sil-va-nee-ya!" he echoed, amending his pronunciation.

"Yes, we're Pennsylvanians," she said, and following her lead, Harry nodded elaborately.

That settled, the Indian launched into his message. He held up one hand with the five fingers spread, then the other with two fingers. *"She-man-thee,"* he said. *"Ne-so-thway She-man-thee."*

"Seven—seven something," Harry muttered.

"Wa-chee-nee-ya." Again he held up seven fingers, peering close to see if they understood. Harry was still mystified, but Sukey had a kind of gift for this. "Virginia!" she exclaimed. "Seven Virginians."

"Ah, ah, ah." Then he pantomimed the act of paddling, the act of creeping through the forest, the act of raising a gun and aiming at the Warrilows.

"Seven Virginians are traveling up here to attack us? Is that what he's trying to say?"

"It must be, Harry. What else could it mean?"

"Some of Connolly's crew, I reckon. But why us?"

"Maybe they're not after us, Harry. Maybe they're after Mr. MacBain."

That could well be. Harry remembered that angry confrontation between Connolly and MacBain over the forge.

"Well, whatever it is, it won't help just standing here," Sukey said. She drew the bar from the door, waggled for Showanyaw to come in, and blew up the fire. By its dancing light, the Indian's painted countenance looked more frightful than ever, but he seemed oblivious to the effect it had. His message delivered, he hunkered down before the blaze and contentedly ate the johnnycake she stirred up for him. He submitted good-humoredly to her examination of his healed arm, allowing her to flex it and feel for the knitted spots in the bones. Harry watched them idly, his mind puzzling over the Indian's message.

What else could his pantomime have meant? That firing a gun, did it have to mean an attack? Maybe the Virginians were just coming here to enlist him in the militia. Or to go hunting, No, no, Showanyaw must have been convinced that the Warrilows were in danger, or he would not have gone out of his way to bring them a midnight warning.

And not only the middle of the night, either, Harry reminded himself. That warpaint might not have portended death and scalping for him and Sukey, but it surely indicated that someone was destined to be attacked. Showanyaw had obviously left a war party to carry this message to their door.

So, the long-predicted rising was taking place at last.

"Sukey," he said, "I'd best warn MacBain."

As he stepped over to the other cabin, he glanced hastily around the clearing. His treasures would have to be taken into the cabin for safekeeping. He rapped, and the door was instantly opened. MacBain had heard them and was alert.

"Seven Virginians?" he echoed when Harry had told his tale. "How does this here Injun come to know 'bout it?"

"I don't know. You speak a little Indian. Why don't you question him?"

" 'Little' is the big word there. But I can try."

Showanyaw leaped up at the sight of MacBain, but he seemed to know who he was. He pointed at him and mimicked the act of pounding. "That's me, right enough," the smith said, then essayed a few stumbling words in Delaware. That was supposed to be close to Shawnee.

Eagerly Showanyaw poured out a stream of language, accompanying it with pantomime of creeping and peering. "Near as I can figger," MacBain reported, "he and his friends was prowlin' through the woods south of here, and they come on these here seven white men 'round a campfire. One of his friends could understand white man's talk, and he reported that the men was on the way to raid two Pennsylvanians who lives up here. He reckoned they meant you."

"It must be us. But does he have an idea *why* they're coming?"

MacBain put the question, but the Indian simply shook his head.

"Well, thank him for us, will you?"

When MacBain had relayed thanks, Showanyaw made a comparatively long speech in return. "I ain't got it all," the smith reported, "but it's somethin' 'bout repayin' a debt."

"Sukey set his broken arm. Could that be it?"

"Mebbe. He don't want to owe nothin' to no white man, he says, 'cause he's on the warpath, and he has to keep his hate up hot."

"Showanyaw!" Sukey cried, shocked.

Harry was startled, too, and yet not altogether surprised. He had known at first sight that this was not the same person as his crony of last fall. "Tell him I don't want him to hate me. Tell him all the things he taught me, they more than make up for the arm. Tell him now we're in *his* debt."

"He says no. He says he don't hate his brother."

"Then there's one more thing I want him to know. Last fall when we quarreled, I—I wouldn't let him have any whiskey. Tell him I wouldn't have denied him if I hadn't reckoned the whiskey would hurt him."

MacBain translated that as best he could and came back with the reply "That there is understood, he says. He was foolish that day. His brothers told him that that there white man was his friend. He don't blame his brother no more. He thanks his brother."

Something that had bothered Harry in a small, nagging way evaporated, and he found himself smiling. The Indian volunteered another speech, and as MacBain listened, a look of satisfaction spread over his face. "He says the Injuns ain't makin' war on Pennsylvania, only on Virginia. What did I tell y'all? He says the Injuns has been murdered all up and down the Ohio, and they has to be scalps took in revenge. He says them seven men comin' here, his party wanted to kill them right off, only they was long knives and outnumbered him and his friends."

"What does he mean by long knives?"

"Backwoods toughs." He snapped his fingers. "By gorries, iffen I ain't got a right good notion of who's aheadin' this raidin' party!"

As he said it, Harry guessed too. "Simon Girty!"

"Right. He didn't do nothin' all last summer but cuss you out and swear he was goin' to have his revenge."

For once Harry was limply glad that the brawny MacBain was here and on their side. Even so, he didn't relish facing Girty and six others of like sort, all alone in the wilderness with no authority but the rifles in their hands. "What do you reckon they have in mind?"

"Well," said MacBain with a wary cock of the head,

"they could kill you and make it look like a Injun raid. But I don't reckon they'd bring that many men iffen it was out-and-out murder they was after."

"What then?"

MacBain shrugged. "Burn your cornfields mebbe. Steal some pigs. Pull down your chimney."

Harry began to swell with anger, and that displaced some fear. Threaten his farm, would they? Not while he breathed! "We'll have to stand siege, I reckon," he said. His head was suddenly sharp and clear and authoritative. It organized things rapidly. "This is the stouter cabin. Do you want to move in here?"

"And leave my forge and tools to them no 'counts? Not me. We defend both cabins."

Showanyaw was showing signs of getting ready to leave. He said something to Harry that MacBain was too abstracted to translate, but it had a good-byeish sound to it. He stepped out into the bright moonlight, and Harry followed him. They touched hands, and the Indian vanished into the forest.

Harry stood looking after him a moment, then ducked back inside. They had a lot to do before Girty and his ruffians arrived.

11

Home Defense

By dawn they had brought all tools and movables inside the cabin, filled every barrel and keg with water and brought them inside, too, and blocked off the chimneys with iron bars. Then MacBain went down to the mouth of the Olethey to keep watch while the Warrilows went about their usual chores.

Nothing happened all morning. Harry reasoned that Showanyaw's party must have come upon the Virginians at the place where they were camped for the night. So, they were probably a good half day's journey away. And so it proved. MacBain reported in for dinner, then was just starting back to his watching place when he halted, staring down the creek.

"They's here!" he called. "Take cover."

Harry and Sukey dashed into their cabin and barricaded the door. Harry then undid the window shutter and opened it a crack to see out. The smithy door was just closing, leaving the clearing empty and ominously waiting.

Harry's heart pounded with excitement, and it came to him with some surprise that—for the moment anyway —he was enjoying himself.

"Any sight of them yet?" Sukey asked anxiously.

"Not— Yes, here they come."

It was Simon Girty all right, burly and unshaven as ever, and behind him came six others more or less the same sort. "Where is they?" one demanded of Girty. "Ain't nobody here."

"Mebbe they went off to Kittanning."

"Iffen so, we got a right good surprise for them when they comes home, hey, Si?"

"Surely do!" They all burst out into their usual guffaws, whacking each other boisterously on the shoulder.

"Well now, let's us go see what they got in them cabins," Girty said. "I'll take this here one, and, George, you take the one with the stone chimney."

Harry closed the shutter and barred it and leaned against the door. Sukey had lighted the betty lamp, and by its dim flame they stared at one another. Harry could barely suppress a grin.

Girty's voice came from only a few feet away: "The latch string ain't out. *They's in there!*" And suddenly there was the most tremendous pounding on the cabin door. "Warrilow, you in there?"

"Yes, I am. What are you here for?"

"To take possession of my propitty."

Thunderstruck, Harry goggled at his sister. "What did you say?"

"I says, to take possession of my propitty. I got a title deed here, signed by Captain John Connolly, magistrate for the county of West Augusta, that says this here land is mine."

But it made no sense. Miles and miles of empty wilderness, and Girty had come to claim *their* land.

"We have an earlier deed," Harry said.

"You come from the East, greenhorn. That there's a Pennsylvania deed, ain't it?"

"Yes, it is. Signed by Governor Penn himself."

"Then it ain't no good. Only Virginia law holds here."

"Nobody's sure of that. I'm not budging."

There was a kind of pause. Harry could hear Girty whispering with his cronies, evidently trying to decide what to do. "Girty?" he called.

"I'm here, greenhorn."

"Why do you want *this* place? Plenty of land on all sides."

"Not land with no salt spring."

A great light dawned on Harry. The salt spring. Of course! Word of their good fortune must have spread through Pittsburgh last winter. This was Girty's chance to get hold of a valuable bit of property and take revenge at the same time.

The whispering resumed while Harry and Sukey stared at one another. They were really in a bad fix. If the men chose, they could simply camp out. Sooner or later the Warrilows would have to leave the cabin. And then, because they were outnumbered by ruthless men, they would be driven from their farm, their sweat-won farm, and no court would back them up.

The whispering stopped, and they heard footsteps approaching the cabin. "Here," said a rough voice, "give you a boost." Someone grunted, and then there was a scrabbling sound overhead.

"Trying the chimney," Harry said.

Sure enough, a voice soon called down from the

rooftop, "They's a bar of some kind blockin' it, Si. You want the chimney throwed down?"

"No, I aim to keep the cabin."

Harry heard the climber slide down the shakes and jump to the ground. Why, he wondered, didn't they block the chimney and smoke him out? Well, the Warrilows had to have some good luck.

There was more pounding on the door. "Greenhorn, you come outen there, or I'll break down the door."

Someone shouted in the distance. Girty yelled back, "Lookee here, Anse MacBain, I ain't got no quarrel with you. You stay out of this here."

MacBain replied, and the answer seemed to give Girty pause. The voices faded, as though they had moved a long way off.

Daringly, Harry slipped over to the shutter, lifted the bar, and opened the leaf a crack. MacBain had found a chink in his smithy walls big enough to admit a gun barrel, and this was now aimed squarely at the Warrilows' door, which he was in an excellent position to cover. Girty and his followers had moved to the far side of the clearing, where they were holding yet another conference.

The conference broke up, the men scattering. Soon rifles were ringing out from all sides, peppering the outsides of both cabins. Evidently Girty thought he'd try what a simple fusillade would do. Harry closed the shutter again and stood with Sukey where there was only solid wall.

"Ball won't penetrate solid wood," he said reassuringly.

"Then why are they using it?"

"Trying to get on our nerves, I reckon. Actually, we're better off for it, because they're using up ammunition. If we can outlast them, we can easily drive them away."

Evidently Girty thought of that, too, for the firing soon fell off. When Harry peered out again, he saw the seven gathered for another conference. Then, while two of them started building a fire, Girty approached the cabin. Just as he was closing the shutter, Harry caught a glimpse of MacBain's muzzle swinging toward the approaching Girty, but there was no report.

Girty pounded on their door again. "Greenhorn, I'm acountin' to ten, and that there's exactly how long you got to come out of there afore I sets fire to the place."

Harry didn't answer.

"One!"

"Sukey," Harry said, soft, "get the old fowling piece."

"Two!"

"Good. Now stand by the shutter, and be prepared to slam it shut the minute I've fired."

"Three!"

"Then I'll give you the rifle to reload and take the fowling piece."

"Four!"

"Then we'll alternate. Understand?"

"Yes."

"Five!"

"Are you going to shoot them, Harry?"

"Six!"

"If they try to fire the house, yes." He looked at her. "Will that bother you?"

"Seven!"

"No, certainly not. Anybody who'd try to take our place from us!" Her gray eyes blazed as she rammed wadding into the ancient gun.

"Eight!"

"Good. Now stand by." He opened the shutter a crack

just as Girty yelled, "Nine!" and knelt by the window, rifle barrel ready to be thrust out.

"Ten! All right, greenhorn, the cabin goes. Come on along." He gestured, and several of his men came running with firebrands. They were heading around the side of the cabin, to the blind back side, but Harry had just time to take aim at the leading one and hit him in the leg. Sukey slammed the shutter closed, barred it, and gave Harry the fowling piece.

"How can we get at them back there?" he demanded, thinking furiously. They had built the cabin too stout. No chinks. But what about the garret? He leaped for the peg ladder and climbed to the loft. Another rifle spoke, and outside someone cursed. Either MacBain was getting in some target practice or the men were shooting each other, because that sounded like a hit.

No, there were no chinks in the loft either. What about the shakes? Because of MacBain, they had had enough nails to nail the roofing to the purlins, instead of just holding it in place with logs, but Harry could probably free one by ramming it with a gun butt. That would leave a loophole in their defense, a place where Girty's men might slip in, but if the smoke that was rapidly filling the garret was any indication, they soon would not have much to defend anyway.

Harry picked his shake, poised his fowling-piece butt for one hard blow, and rammed with all his strength. As the shake flew up, he thrust his head through the opening. Three of Girty's men were piling boughs on a blaze already crackling away merrily against the back wall of the cabin. Harry aimed at their legs and pulled the trigger, then without waiting to see what effect the shot had had, he ducked down inside again.

Sukey held up the reloaded rifle, and he handed down the fowling piece and dashed back to his opening. Two of the men were bending over a third, who sat on the ground, nursing his knee. When Harry reappeared, they moved hastily back around the corner of the house.

He pointed the rifle at the wounded man. "Pull that fire away from the house," he said grimly, "or this goes straight to the head."

"How'm I s'posed to move a fire," he complained. "I got a ball in my leg."

"And you're going to have one in your head if you don't pull that fire away."

Groaning, the man hitched himself closer to the blaze

and with a stick knocked the burning faggots free of the house wal' It was already afire in one spot, and Harry ordered the man to beat out the flames, which he did with his stick.

Girty appeared. "Here, what you doin' there, Will—?" He glanced up, saw Harry, and his rifle shot to his shoulder. Harry ducked back inside half a second ahead of a bullet.

The other men had gone to fetch their rifles, too, and from now on, they'd have some keep guard while the others built the fire. Harry sat on the loft floor, trying to think. He could put the rifle out, hold it one-handed over the edge, and kind of fire down in the general direction of where the men would be working. There was a risk he might drop the gun from the recoil, but it would keep him from exposing himself. Make them jumpy even if he didn't hit anyone.

But these stopgap measures were only postponements. However they strained themselves with one desperate defense and then another, Girty had only to come back again. Time was on his side. They had to do more than prevent him from burning down their cabin. They had to drive him away.

But how? Strike fear into him? What was he afraid of? The answer was discouragingly obvious: nothing on God's green earth.

Sukey appeared in the ladder opening with the reloaded fowling piece. "What's happening?"

"Well, I winged another one. If that yell I heard a few minutes ago means anything, we've laid up three of them altogether."

"Good."

"It doesn't seem to have discouraged them any. Listen."

The cries were all "Come on now, hustle up that there firewood. . . . Blow it up. . . . Got it cracklin' good now. . . ." Soon smoke began to seep under the edges of the roof again.

Harry preferred risking the fowling piece to risking the rifle, so he handed Sukey the rifle and took the other weapon, lay down on the floor, and wiggled over until he was under the loose shake. Then, taking as firm a grip on the weapon as he could, he slid it out the opening, pointed downward, and fired.

The recoil all but broke his arm, but the measure was effective. There was an outcry and some vigorous cursing, and Girty shouted, "We're goin' to git you for that, greenhorn. We're comin' in right now."

"Come ahead," Harry called back. "We have two guns and can shoot as fast as you can squeeze through the opening."

There was a short silence. Then one of the other men said, "Now, lookee here, Si Girty, I didn't join this here expedition to git myself kilt. 'Come on and help me run some greenhorn outen the new lands'—that there's what you said. That last ball whistled past me so close it like to've shave a line through my whiskers."

"Yep . . . that's right . . ." the other men said. "And not even no scalps neither."

"They's York County scum, is all. Y'all want them pig-keepin' farmers livin' in Virginia?"

"Way off up here, they ain't likely to bother me none at all."

"And the salt spring. I tell y'all, they ain't no other salt works nearer'n Big Bone Lick in Kaintuck, and that there is bad Shawnee and Cherokee country. I tell y'all, we're goin' to be rich."

"I say wait it out. No sense takin' a risk when a little waitin' will git you the same thing."

And so they argued it out, and finally the men had it their way. As the arguing voices faded in the distance, Harry slipped out through the loose shingle, threw dirt on the rekindled fire, and nipped around to the door where Sukey hastily let him in.

They ate their supper in peace, then as dusk settled over the clearing, there was a light rapping at the door. "It's me, Anse."

Harry let him in, relieved and delighted to see his curly black head and big white grin. It wasn't so bad when there were three of them.

"I reckoned it was safer for me to come out than y'all, so I come over to spend the night."

"I'm glad you did," said Harry. "We've got to talk, to think of some way to get rid of them."

"Why's they here in the fust place? Did y'all find out?"

"Yes, he's come to seize the property—has a Virginia deed and all. He wants it for the salt spring."

Even MacBain went a bit slackjawed at that news. "Why, that ain't done. A man don't take another man's land. Lessen it's some smart-talkin' lawyer man from back East."

"Outside there are seven men trying to do it."

"A tomahawk claim's enough to hold a piece of ground. Y'all got a deed from the Penns. No man in the new lands jumps another man's claim—it plain ain't done. How does Girty come to have six men willin' to do it?"

Harry stared at the smith, struck with an idea. "Would a tomahawk claim mean more to them than a written deed?"

"It might."

"Because this land has been blazed. We did it, Kaspar and I, at the time we first found it."

"By gorries," said the smith, rubbing his chin, "you might have a idee there. Tomorrow I'll go down to their campfire and talk to them. Iffen his men leaves, they ain't much Girty can do agin the three of us."

They were pretty well tired out, after having been up most of the previous night, but they didn't think it was safe for all of them to go to sleep, so they divided the night into three watches and kept alert.

Only one incident disturbed the night. It was during Harry's watch, which he passed sitting in front of the loose shake, rifle across his knees. He thought he heard —something. The faintest possible change in air pressure that meant that nearby some thing was moving. Then slowly, the shake was lifted up and up until light entered—for it was bright moonlight again—and then slowly, slowly higher until a man's head was framed in the opening.

Harry raised the rifle. "You know a loaded gun when you see one, I hope," he said.

The face disappeared.

Harry was afraid to risk looking out to make sure, but he thought the man was Girty himself.

After that they were left undisturbed, and in the morning, after breakfast, MacBain went down to the campfire to try to talk the men into abandoning Girty.

He came back an hour later, shaking his head. "Girty has them all to thinkin' they's goin' to get rich from salt boilin'. They good as own that a tomahawk claim did ought to be final, but they's stayin' jest the same."

Harry sighed. "If only there were something they were afraid of—really afraid."

MacBain glanced up, surprised. "Why, they's plenty of things they's scairt of," he objected.

"Oh?"

"Hants, for one."

"Hants?"

"Spooks, ghosts. They don't cotton much to witchcraftin' neither. And naturally they's scairt of smallpox and the ague."

"Spooks," Harry said slowly. "Do you reckon we could make them believe this place is haunted or cursed in some fashion."

"Better yet," Sukey put in, "tell them I'm a witch and have put a curse on them. If they don't believe you, ask them how we knew they were coming."

12
New Relations

MacBain looked troubled. "That there's a risky business, Miss Susannah—givin' yourself a name for witchin'. Later on, it could mebbe git you blamed for somethin' that ain't nobody's fault."

"Nonsense!" Sukey said crisply. She was always willing to let the future take care of itself. "It's only taking advantage of their ignorance."

Harry wasn't altogether happy about the idea either, for Sukey's sake or his own—hiding behind her skirts. But it did seem the most feasible scheme. "We have to try *something*," he said.

"Then it's settled," she said. "Now how shall we go about it? Images, I think."

She whipped up a pasty dough of cornmeal and barley and molded seven human figures out of it. She made them good and big so they could be seen from afar, and hence she had to bake them one at a time in the bake kettle.

By noon they were ready. MacBain volunteered to set them up. He slipped out through the loose shake and nailed up the seven "dolls" in a row along the rooftree. He then took seven splinters of wood that Harry had prepared and drove a "stake" through the heart of each doll. He returned inside to report that his activities had attracted the attention of the men lounging by a campfire along the brook and that they would doubtless be up to ask questions shortly.

And so it proved. Soon they heard the mutter of voices outside the cabin, and there was the usual pounding at the door. "Greenhorn, answer me."

"What do you want, Girty?"

"Them—things on your roof. What is they?"

"Witch dolls. They stand for you and your friends. My sister made them. She's a well-known witch, you know."

They all grinned at one another as they waited to see how that would go down. Nothing at all happened for a minute or two. Then Girty said, "Aaaagh, that there's a lot of hogwash. She ain't no witch."

"Oh, isn't she? Then how is it we knew you were coming hours before you got here—in plenty of time to prepare?"

That, too, caused silence, and the men began to murmur: "They *did* know . . . they was all prepared . . . how could they unless . . . ?"

"The witch dolls put a terrible curse on you—all seven of you. If you linger here on the Olethey, you will slowly wither away and die. The only way you can escape it is to go away, leave this area entirely!"

"She ain't no witch," Girty said again but feebly.

"She sells herbs and simples," one of his men offered. "I seen her in Pittsburgh. And that's what witches does."

"Yep, and how's come we can't get in there? And ever'

time they shoots they hits one of us. You keep talkin' 'bout greenhorns. Greenhorns doesn't shoot that good. Not lessen they has—help."

"Into each one of these dolls," Harry said, drawing on his imagination, "has been baked a curse. A baked-in curse cannot be removed by another person. It lasts as long as the accursed person lives."

Outside, the mutterings grew louder and louder until the men were shouting at each other angrily. "That there's just a trick to drive us away. Y'all lettin' a pig farmer trick you outen your propitty."

"I ain't takin' no chances with no curse."

"Me neither."

"They ain't nothin' to them dolls but dough. Lookee here, boost me up, and I'll pull one off and show y'all."

"Not me. I ain't havin' nothin' to do with no witch dolls. I'm aleavin'. Comin', George?"

The dispute faded off down toward the brook. Harry unbarred the shutter and peered out. The men had come in two elm-bark canoes, and one was now being reembarked. Girty expostulated with the departing men, but they paid no attention. Two of the four who were leaving limped, using saplings for crutches, and a third carried his left arm in a sling. Soon they had loaded their belongings aboard and were paddling off down the Olethey. That left Girty with only two followers.

Still, that was two more than Harry liked to see, and when the remaining two seemed to be continuing the argument, he silently encouraged them. Finally, after an hour or more, the remaining boat was launched, the two remaining followers and at last—reluctantly—Girty himself climbed aboard and pushed off.

With vast sighs of relief, the Warrilows flung open door

and window and surveyed their rescued acres. Beyond a bit of trampling here and there, the Girty party had not even damaged them much.

They held a short orgy of hugging one another, clapping each other on the shoulder, and shaking hands. Harry felt oddly brilliant, pleased with himself. He had fought off Girty and outwitted him as well. Confidence surged through him.

He even found himself grinning fondly at MacBain. The smith had backed them up all the way, had made their quarrel his quarrel. If he wanted to marry Sukey, well, he'd earned the right.

But in the midst of all this rejoicing, Harry had a chilly second thought. "Do you reckon Girty can find some new men? Ones who aren't so superstitious?"

"Wal, now that's hard to say. Not soon, anyways. Lookee how long it took him to get this here crew together."

True. It was five months since their visit to Pittsburgh.

" 'Sides, they's gettin' ready to go after the Injuns —mebbe they's even set out a'ready. And Girty's a lieutenant in the militia. They's goin' to need ever' man iffen they mean to go for the Shawnee."

"We'll never be rid of him unless I can get that deed torn up. Do you reckon there's any chance I can talk Connolly into canceling it?"

MacBain shook his black head. "That there's a powerful prideful man. He ain't never goin' to admit he was wrong 'bout something'."

"I reckon I ought to try," Harry insisted. "I'm going to Pittsburgh. Just as soon as I've boiled out enough salt to pay for the trip."

"Oh, Harry, no!" Sukey cried. "Girty and his ruffians will half-kill you!"

"I'm safer in Pittsburgh than here. He wouldn't do anything before witnesses."

"You might run into an Indian war party. Think what Showanyaw said."

"That could just as well happen right here. No, I've got to make the attempt."

"Then put it off until fall," Sukey insisted. "Take whiskey and salt to market and then ask. If they're planning an expedition, they will need salt and whiskey both."

"That there's a good idee, Miss Susannah," MacBain said enthusiastically. "Harry, you wait till fall, then offer to sell the produce to the troops iffen they'll call off Girty's deed."

"By then the whole thing may be over."

"Even so, Harry, you won't be arguing with empty hands."

Gradually Harry let them persuade him.

Two days after the Girty party had left, while Harry was busily hollowing out logs for kegs, MacBain came up to him. They were well out of earshot of the house, but the smith spoke so low that it was almost a whisper. "I been meanin' to talk to you, Harry."

Harry straightened and stretched to ease his back. "Yes? What about?"

"It's 'bout Miss Susannah."

"Oh?" Despite his changed feelings toward the smith, Harry felt a renewed pang. "What about Sukey?"

But MacBain seemed to stick at that point. His air,

usually bursting with all-conquering self-confidence, seemed now rather defeated.

"What is it, Anse? What about Sukey?"

"She plain won't let me tell her I love her!" MacBain burst out. "She—she likes me—I reckon. But ever' time I go to hold her hand and say sweet things, she stops me. No, I mustn't, she says, she don't want to fall in love with me."

A month ago, Harry would have found that pure good news—even now he was conscious of a certain lightness of heart. But his chief feeling was puzzlement.

"So I wanted to ask if it was on account of you," MacBain went on. "Are you workin' agin me?"

"No, of course not!" Harry said indignantly. "It's not my affair to decide who she marries."

"Is it on *account* of you—I mean, mebbe she feels she should give up her own life for you."

Harry pondered. He was used to being Sukey's favorite and all, but he had never gotten the impression that she intended to sacrifice her life for his. "I don't *think* so."

"It's like she tooken a vow to stay a single woman," the smith said, perplexed. "I axed her oncet was that it, and she said no."

"I've never—never talked to her about you. But I'll ask if you want."

MacBain looked relieved, as though that's what he'd been trying to request all along. "You do that for me?"

"Well, certainly. I owe you a bigger favor than that."

But it turned out to be not such a small favor after all, for Harry found it extremely difficult to get up the nerve. In the next few days, there were at least three occasions when he was alone with his sister, and neither of them was too busy to have a talk, and he funked it each time. Finally, while they were hoeing one day in neighboring rows of corn, he took a deep breath and plunged in.

"Sukey, how do you feel about Anse?"

She did not glance up from her work. After a minute, she answered stiffly, "Mr. MacBain has been a good friend."

"Yes, he has, but that isn't what I asked you."

"Really, Harry, what is this about?"

"He wants to marry you, Sukey—you know that perfectly well. As your only male relative"—he knew he was sounding like an ass, but there seemed no other way to sound—"I reckon I ought to know the—the state of your feelings about this man."

"I've told you. I like him. He's been good to us. I won't let it go further than that."

"Why not?"

There was a long, long pause. "I have my reasons."

"I'll be switched if I can think what they are."

Another silence. Then abruptly she gave an answer for which he was totally unprepared: "He keeps slaves."

Harry blinked. Slaves? Then he remembered Belle and Maynard. "His housekeeper, you mean?"

"And her son. The father is still back in Virginia. Anse couldn't afford to buy him too."

Harry's surprise vanished almost as quickly as it had come. He should have thought of that for himself. Sukey was something of a fanatic on the subject of slavery. She had been friend and pupil of an old former slave, had learned all her herb growing and doctoring from the little black woman. Once she had taken Harry, while they were in Philadelphia, to a meeting of the Anti-Slavery Society, a newly formed Quaker group. There they had heard lurid tales of families broken up, floggings, cruel practices of various sorts, of one man owning a hundred of his fellowmen, another owning over three hundred, and so on. (Harry was a bit skeptical about that last; he didn't see how one man could own and get work out of three hundred others without a certain amount of cooperation on their part. On the whole, he decided, he would be against slavery when slaves were against slavery.) Once reminded of Sukey's passionate hatred, it was easy for Harry to see why she would not permit MacBain to get close enough to engage her affections.

"Have you told him this?"

"No."

"Why not? If his feelings for you are strong, surely he'd be willing to free them."

"I can't ask that of him." She bent over her hoe so Harry couldn't see her face.

"I don't understand, Sukey."

"Well," she said, "they're valuable. At least Belle is. She told me once that she cost forty-five pounds—that's nearly twice what our whole farm is worth. She isn't just a common field hand, she said, but a fully trained house servant."

An eerie feeling passed over Harry. Fancy knowing your exact worth in pounds, shillings, and pence! The very price you would bring in the open market! Harry didn't think he would fetch anything near as much as forty-five pounds.

He passed off the feeling with a shiver. "Don't you reckon you should let Anse decide whether you're worth such a loss to him?"

She mumbled something he couldn't hear.

"What did you say?"

"Oh, Harry, don't try to do me a favor!" she exploded. "I know what I'm doing!" She resumed her hoeing with furious energy and moved away so rapidly that soon he was facing her back.

He stared after her suspiciously. Was she afraid? Sukey, who feared nothing in the world but Indians, was she afraid of being put to the test? Afraid that MacBain, with a clear-cut choice, would take his servants instead of her? He remembered his own reluctance, right up to this minute, to ask her how she felt.

He knew then that she *was* in love. Nobody whose feelings were only lukewarm would shrink from such a test.

Now that the thing that he'd dreaded had actually come to pass, he found it not so very terrible at all. But her behavior put him in an unpleasant dilemma. Should he tell MacBain and thus force the test upon her whether she

would or not? Or should he remain hands off—stand back
and allow her to choose unhappiness?

For a day or two longer, he managed to avoid MacBain,
but inevitably the smith cornered him at last. "You axed
her yit?"

Harry gazed at him unhappily. "She told me," he said at
last, "but she made me promise not to tell you."

"Not tell me?" MacBain echoed, dumbfounded.

"It's nothing to do with you personally, Anse. The fact
is—well, I reckon maybe she is a bit sweet on you. But she
has her reasons for not wanting to give in to her feelings."

A smile started creeping over MacBain's face as soon as
Harry said he thought Sukey was fond of him, and with a
return of his old self-confidence, he dismissed the rest as
of no importance. "She likes me—I knowed it!" he cried,
slapping his knee. "Wal, now, I reckon I can take it up
from there. Thank you a right heap, Harry. You made a
new man out of me."

"No, wait, Anse. Don't go off half-cocked. Listen to me."

"The ladies, they gits notional sometimes, but they
comes 'round in the end."

"You're making a mistake, Anse. Sukey is the last
person in the world to act flighty. This—this thing, it's
terribly important to her."

"Sure it is. I ain't sayin' it ain't. But they's other things
more important, and I aims to show her what they is."

"Anse, don't be a fool. You don't know Sukey one bit if
you think you can sweet-talk her out of her principles."

"Harry, you're a mite young yit. Principles doesn't last
long in the moonlight."

Harry gazed at him grimly. "Anse, a couple of days ago,
you asked if I was working against you. Well, if I were, I'd
encourage you not to take Sukey's notions seriously."

"How am I s'posed to take somethin' serious when you won't tell me what-all it is?"

"You'll have to take my word. There's something holding my sister back from giving herself to you, and the very fact that she does—well, that she does have feelings for you and still holds back, that ought to show you that this—this thing is important to her."

MacBain didn't look very convinced, but he said he wouldn't rush Sukey, and Harry had to be satisfied with that.

13
Lord Dunmore

At first, as far as Harry could tell, the smith was cautious enough in his wooing. It was flax-harvesting time anyway, and they were all so busy that there was little time for courtship or even for brooding about Girty. The plants had to be pulled up by the roots, then alternately dried and soaked until they were ready for breaking—an endless and exhausting job. Despite the hard work, Sukey sang all day long. Flax breaking meant she would soon be spinning again, and she loved to spin. Harry would have a wheel made for her when he went to Pittsburgh in the fall.

But MacBain must have put his foot in it somehow, for toward summer's end they quarreled. Harry came in from the field one day and found Sukey tight-lipped and pink-faced, making rather more clatter, as she prepared supper, than was absolutely necessary. When Harry said, "What's wrong? Why are you angry?" she snapped, "Nothing's wrong! Leave me alone."

MacBain did not show up for supper, and the following day, instead of working at his anvil, he vanished into the woods, and they could hear him savagely chopping down trees. Well, Harry thought, wincing as yet another trunk was heard crashing down, the land has to be cleared eventually anyway.

There was coldness between Sukey and the smith for days and days, and Harry told himself privately that if they did marry, it was sure to be a stormy relationship. Had she asked MacBain to free Belle? If so, obviously he had refused. But somehow Harry didn't think she had. MacBain had just stepped over some invisible barrier that Sukey had laid down—barriers that women are always erecting and expecting men to know about without being told. (Harry had walked out with a few girls back in Lancaster County and felt very woman-wise.)

Except for that the summer was eventless. They saw no more of Girty or of anyone else, except a passing trader, who had no news for them. It was a hot summer, and they had a bumper crop of corn, so that Harry's chief problem was to provide enough containers for the whiskey and salt they were to sell. What with that and the kettles and other items MacBain was taking to Pittsburgh, they decided to travel by river and built a huge raft.

Impatient to get to the town, Harry distilled as early as he reasonably could and was ready to leave by mid-September. He had seven kegs of whiskey and three of salt, and he had begun to toy with the notion of buying a yoke of oxen.

He and MacBain set off early one hot day. The water was low in the Olethey, and the raft grounded several times on gravel banks before they reached the deeper Allegheny. Then there was nothing to do but lean back

and watch the wooded hills slip past. In due course, they encountered Fort Pitt and the Monongahela, and having poled up the wider stream, they beached the raft below Water Street.

They found Pittsburgh in an uproar—a kind of cyclone revolving around Captain—now Major—John Connolly. Messengers arrived from Williamsburg in a steady stream, and others just as continuously left Pittsburgh for the Virginia capital. People reported to MacBain that Connolly and his men had spent most of the spring and early summer harassing Pennsylvania magistrates and traders, invading their houses and stores, forcing them to pay

ruinous duties on peltry, and occasionally imprisoning them in the guardhouse at the fort. Pennsylvania, without a militia, could not at first strike back, but finally Arthur St. Clair had organized an informal group of rangers, and thereafter there were fewer incidents.

In June, Connolly had changed the name of Fort Pitt to Fort Dunmore, in honor of his patron, and had posted another proclamation forbidding people to supply the Shawnee with "dangerous commodities." He seemed determined to have an Indian war.

The little Indian encampment across the Allegheny was quite empty, and one of the first items of gossip that Harry and MacBain heard on their arrival was the story of

Connolly's manhunt through town for three Shawnee chieftains. The Shawnee had escorted two Pennsylvania traders through the hostile Ohio country, but not only did Major Connolly refuse to guarantee their safety in Pittsburgh, but he tried to seize and imprison them. Their friends only just managed to smuggle them safely out of town, a few minutes ahead of the Virginians' search party.

There was no question but that war parties were out. From time to time, word came of this settler burned out. that group forting up along the Monongahela. In retaliation, armed parties of whites were sent out now and then to burn Shawnee cornfields and take a few scalps, and Connolly had ordered the building of a fort at Wheeling Creek. Earlier in the summer, he had talked of leading a body of troops himself, to reinforce the men in Fort Wheeling and thence make a full-scale assault on the Shawnee towns in the Ohio country. But now it was said that Dunmore was planning to take over the expedition in person.

As soon as they had beached their raft and been raucously welcomed by some of MacBain's friends, Harry and the smith parted, MacBain heading for his establishment, Harry setting out to find Connolly. Locating him was not a difficult matter, but getting the haughty major to stand still long enough for Harry to pour out his complaint about Girty was something else.

"Lieutenant Girty is a loyal Virginian," the major answered coldly. "He came to me with word of a certain piece of land he wished to occupy, and I permitted him to buy it."

"Did you know that the land was already occupied, sir?"

"I did not. But since the Penns had no business selling land they didn't own, I cannot see that it matters."

Harry had had plenty of time to prepare his argument. He now drew a long breath and launched himself: "Sir, you are making quite a good thing out of selling land, aren't you?"

It is well nigh impossible to look down your nose at someone who is taller than you are, but Major Connolly gave it a jolly good try. "I am acting in the interests of His Majesty's most ancient and loyal colony of Virginia."

"Yes, sir, but what will happen to those sales when word gets out that you are selling occupied land? Many people will wonder what will happen to *their* land if the decision goes against Virginia. They'll tell themselves, Maybe I'll buy this land and clear it and build a cabin, and then later someone will come along with a Pennsylvania deed."

"The decision will not go against Virginia."

"*You* think so, sir, and perhaps you are right. But not everyone is so confident, and people's confidence is what we're talking about."

Harry thought he saw a flicker on the other man's face that indicated some of this was hitting home. But Connolly was too stubborn to change his mind as he proved by saying, "The deed has been issued, the money paid, I cannot rescind that." And when Harry tried to continue his plea, the major impatiently brushed him aside and hurried on back to his uproar making.

What should he do now? Harry wondered. If Lord Dunmore was actually going to be here soon, perhaps it would be worthwhile waiting and speaking to him directly. Harry didn't like the idea much—the frustration of being dependent on the whim of some distant potentate—but he could think of nothing else. He headed for the smithy to see what MacBain thought.

A horde of men had gathered in the smithy yard to welcome MacBain, and so much blacksmithery had piled up in his absence that he already had the forge fire lighted and was hard at work on the first of a long line of guns to be repaired. Everybody seemed to take it for granted that they would soon march out to "chastise" the Shawnee and the Mingo.

But the chief topic among the crowd was not the Indian war but events back East. Major Connolly had been right when he had predicted the government would bitterly resent Boston's destruction of the East India Company's tea. It had demanded that the Massachusetts city pay for the tea, and when Boston refused to come up with a penny, it had passed a series of enactments to punish the town. The port was closed, the Massachusetts seat of government moved to Salem, and the colonial government so reformed that London had much tighter control over it. Men accused of capital crimes could be taken to England for trial, and Regulars under General Thomas Gage were sent to occupy the town.

Harry's first reaction to this news was to pity the soldiers. Boston was not an easy city to occupy, as no one knew better than he, for he had been part of an earlier occupying force himself. "Well," he said reasonably, "why doesn't Boston pay for the tea? She did destroy it, you know."

"That there'd be as good as payin' the tax, man!"

There was a chorus of heated agreement. Pittsburghers all seemed to be hot liberty men and roundly denounced Parliament with one voice. For once Virginians and Pennsylvanians thought alike.

"Them people in London, they got no call tellin' us what to do, tryin' to put taxes on us," one man fumed. "Now look what theys doin' to Boston—gettin' *more* power over them! And closin' the port—why, from what I hear tell, that's as good as starvin' them Boston folk. And they can do it 'cause they got the power."

"Yep . . . that there's right . . . that's what they done . . ." the rest sputtered.

But all that was far off and made Harry a trifle impatient. What was Boston to him? He'd turned his back on the East. And then a newcomer stepped forward.

"And you know what else they done?" he said importantly.

He had evidently just returned from the East, for they all swung around toward him, eager for fresh news: "What? What?"

"They says the Ohio is now the border of Canady."

Silence. Everyone looked at everyone else.

"What they mean by that?" someone ventured.

"They's achangin' the map," the newcomer insisted. "They run Canady right down on top of us, sayin' Ohio River is the boundary. Them as is tradin' in Ohio country, they's in Canady."

It was something called the Quebec Act. The way the newcomer told it, London had taken away Canada's general assembly and swelled her borders to the Ohio line. Ontario, Erie, all the Great Lakes were to be Canada from now on.

"But—but, good lack, can the government *do* that?" Harry cried. "Sit over there in Parliament and—and just move the map of America around?"

"They claims they can." He whipped out a Philadelphia paper and pointed to the paragraph that described the new act.

Harry took it in dreamlike fashion and in dreamlike

fashion spelled out the story. It was all there, just as the man had said. Still, he felt compelled to say, "I can't believe it."

For the first time, all this talk of liberty and Boston's troubles and what London was trying to do to the colonies struck home to Harry. Come to that, he'd felt a slight chill over that "taken to England for trial" part, too. But this map business wasn't some abstract thing. He knew the Ohio, he knew the Allegheny. If he glanced up, he could see them. What had some distant Colonial Office lordling to do with *his* country?

Indignation began to stir in him—some of what, he assumed, the others had felt all along. It wasn't right that people in far-off places should have control of his life, his property. People ought to run things themselves, the way that they knew to be right for them. Ohio River the border of Canada indeed! It was ridiculous.

"But folks ain't just sittin' still for it neither," the trader resumed, pleased to be the center of an avid crowd. "They's called a meetin'—all the colonies to send representatives to a big meetin' in Philadelphy. Congress they's callin' it—a continental congress."

Mention something like that to an American, Harry had found, and right away he started talking politics. The excited buzz was instantaneous. Was Pittsburgh to be represented, and if so, by whom? Names were tossed in the air, and the split between Pennsylvania advocates and those of Virginia became apparent once more. But politics did not interest Harry, so he left the group and went inside the smithy where MacBain was hard at work.

"Connolly said no," Anse guessed the minute he saw Harry's glum face.

"Eh? Oh, yes, he says the papers are issued and can't be recalled. Anse, have you heard about this Ohio River business?"

"Ohio River?"

Harry explained. MacBain had a piece of gun lock on the anvil, but it paled and cooled as he stood unmoving, staring at Harry. At last he said gruffly, "They ain't never goin' to make *that* stick." He came to himself and, realizing that the piece of iron was too cold to work, thrust it back in the fire. "What do them London people think they's up to?" he inquired, perplexed. "Why, Virginny's charter takes her all the way to the Great South Sea. Parliament can't meddle with a King's charter."

"It's part of this Boston affair."

"Then we got to support Boston."

It was certainly beginning to look that way.

"Well," said MacBain, returning to more immediate business, "what you goin' to do 'bout Connolly."

Harry sighed. "Dunmore himself is coming to town soon. I'd thought of appealing to him. He had no part in the land sale, so he doesn't have to admit to being wrong. It would be easy enough for him to do away with the deed."

The metal was white hot again. MacBain lifted it with his tongs to the anvil and began to tap. "Worth a try," he said.

"How long a wait do you reckon it will be?"

"Not long. Call's out a'ready for the Virginia militia."

"The militia? Wasn't it called up last winter? That's what all the fuss was about."

"That there was the militia of the Pittsburgh region. Now Dunmore's callin' out the whole frontier."

"Oh?"

"Feller who owns this here gun, he left Winchester a week ago, and the word was then that the gov'nor was to march in two more days. He may be here any day now."

As it happened, their wait was no more than a few hours, for that very evening, the Virginians came wading across the Monongahela at the Turtle Creek ford and marched in by Braddock's road.

Harry let the governor go while he took care of his first responsibility: hunting out the commissary officer in order to sell his whiskey and salt. He located the man all right, and he was willing to buy two kegs of whiskey and one of salt, but he wanted to pay Harry in tobacco notes.

"I don't smoke," Harry objected. "I have no use for tobacco."

"You don't get the leaf itself, just a note saying how much you own."

"It's still no good to me."

A long, tiresome wrangle ensued. It seemed that in Virginia everything was paid for in tobacco, and the commissary officer really did want the whiskey and salt. After a while Harry had an idea.

"Look here," he said, "I'll let you have the items if your superior—if Lord Dunmore signs something for me."

"*Signs* something? Signs what?"

"A Virginia deed to land I already own. A deed that would make earlier Virginia deeds worthless." That would be the same as buying the land all over again, but peace of mind was worth it.

The officer glared at Harry suspiciously, but after thinking it over, he agreed to go with Harry to talk to the governor. It was dark by then, and the campfires of the Virginians glowed from every hillside around. Many still thronged the streets of the little village or roistered in taverns. There must have been a thousand or more.

"An army," Harry muttered.

"Oh, what's here is only half of us. The southern counties are with Andrew Lewis. We're to rendezvous with them at the Little Kanawha."

"Where's that?"

"Down the Ohio a few miles. Say, you're a likely looking young feller. How about you signing on, too?"

"I'd sooner enlist with the Shawnee."

The officer gaped at Harry, then decided that was a joke and laughed hugely, clapping him on the shoulder.

They found Lord Dunmore in Semple's tavern, seated before the taproom fire and surrounded by what must have been his aides. One even wore some species of military uniform. The group gave off an air of being in a desperate hurry and bustle, but Harry thought that was more for appearance's sake than true busyness. When his commissary officer approached, the governor seemed perfectly free to hear his report.

While the officer explained about the whiskey and the difficulty over using tobacco as a medium of exchange, Harry studied the governor. What he saw was not cheering. Lord Dunmore was a smallish man with a bland, self-satisfied face, and at mention of Harry's making conditions over the sale of his whiskey, he frowned majestically.

"If this fellow will not sell, then seize the supplies," he said. "One can't bargain with peasants."

The officer goggled at the governor. "But, sir—" he said feebly.

"What would you have of me, Edwards? Take what is needed. If necessary, make out an order on the colonial

government for a fair price. It can be presented in Williamsburg for payment."

"Sir," said the officer with an unhappy glance at Harry, "the lad will accept, in lieu of payment, a Virginia deed to land which, he says, he already owns."

"Eh? A deed in lieu of payment? That sounds most irregular."

"Sir, it would—it would antagonize the local population if we simply took possession of the goods." He nudged Harry. "Tell him the details."

Harry produced his Penn deed and explained about Major Connolly's having mistakenly issued a Virginia deed to the same tract of land. "All I want, my lord, is a piece of paper saying that the land is mine and that any earlier Virginia deeds are canceled."

But Lord Dunmore's ear had caught only one name. "Major Connolly issued this Virginia deed, did he? Then it must be correct."

"My lord, he wasn't aware at the time—"

"I place utmost trust in Major Connolly's judgment."

"But, my lord, won't you even investigate—?"

"I *said,*" his lordship repeated, turning a rather attractive shade of purple, "that I place the utmost trust in Major Connolly's judgment." He turned away and addressed one of the other aides.

"Please, my lord, if you would just look into the matter—"

Without glancing in their direction, the governor said, "Take this fellow away, Edwards. Seize his whiskey if he will not listen to reason."

It was plain that, for him, the matter was closed.

14
Possessions

Harry and the commissary officer left Semple's and stood for a moment in the street. The officer was embarrassed. "Sorry about that," he said sheepishly. "Some of these lordships—well, they think it's back in the good old days of 'Chop off his head!' "

"Yes," Harry said.

"I won't be seizing your property, never fear."

"Thanks."

With a light clap on the shoulder, the officer departed, and Harry headed with dragging steps for the smithy. What was he to do now? Wild schemes sped through his imagination: going along on the expedition after all and seizing a chance to put a bullet in Girty . . . forging a deed like the one he'd wanted from Dunmore . . . traveling to London and asking the Colonial Office for help. . . .

Moodily he discarded them one by one. There plain wasn't anything he could do. Not as long as things were set up this way, with distant people—distant in ideas and ways of looking at things as well as distant in space—having control of his life. He found himself suddenly filled with sympathy for Boston. Helpless, that's how Bostonians must feel. Bound and gagged.

MacBain had finished work for the day and was just sitting down to supper, which Belle served with a proud flourish. A place was hastily laid for Harry, and he plopped down heavily across from the smith and described his lack of success.

When he'd finished, the other sighed and sat silent for a while. Then he said, "You and me, Harry, we ain't doin' so good."

"So you did quarrel with Sukey," Harry said, for a moment forgetting his own problems.

"I love that girl, Harry, but I can't let her run me."

In spite of his low feelings, Harry grinned. "She tries to run me, too." There was a long, awkward pause. Then Harry said, "Are you coming back with me?"

"Not only comin' back. I'm takin' up some land of my own—that there stretch atween your propitty and the 'Gheny. Set up a permanent forge there and do a bit of farmin' atween shoein' jobs."

"I'm glad to hear it, Anse, really I am."

"You hear that, Belle. You're agoin' up the river to live. You reckon you'll like it?"

For answer the housekeeper gave a wild, noncommittal cackle, called him Mist' Anse, and bent over her cooking pots.

Harry drew a long breath and expelled it with a gust. As fast as that he came to a big decision: He was going to do Sukey the favor she had begged him not to do. "Anse," he said firmly, "I wouldn't."

"You wouldn't what?"

"Take Belle along. Not at least without changing a couple of things first."

"Changing—?" MacBain suddenly caught the significance that Harry had put into his voice. He frowned. "What you tryin' to tell me?"

"It would be better if Belle—if she weren't—if she had—" How to say it without actually saying it?

MacBain's frown, if anything, deepened. "Does this here that you're tryin' to tell me have anythin' to do with your sister?"

Harry nodded.

MacBain leaned closer and spoke in a low tone. "Are you tryin' to say she don't like Belle?"

"No, no!" Plague take it, the man wasn't *that* dense!

"Then why don't she want her up there?"

"It isn't Belle herself, it's what she represents."

"She don't like black people?"

In exasperation, Harry abandoned the roundabout way he'd been talking. "She hates slavery," he said flatly.

MacBain's mouth formed a round, astonished O, but no sound came out. "But what's she got agin slavery?" he said at last.

"She was befriended once by a former slave. She feels very strongly about it, Anse, very strongly."

"She don't understand. Black people, they can't git along by their own selves. It would be plumb mean of me to turn Belle free. Why, how'd she support herself?"

"Lots of free Negroes support themselves. Look at Mr. Richard, the tavern keeper. Besides, what's wrong with you hiring her, paying wages for her work the way you would any servant?"

"Pay wages? To my own propitty?"

All this conversation was being carried on in the same room with Belle herself, who was pretending to be deaf. Harry called across to her, "Belle, would you like to be free?"

"Why, Mist' Harry, what I do be free?" She laughed shrilly.

"See," said MacBain. "She doesn't even want to be free. She knows better."

"She doesn't think she has a serious chance of being freed, so she's giving you the answer you want."

MacBain sat silent for a long time. Then he said, "I have to think about this here, Harry. I have to think mighty hard."

The following day, Harry went back to Semple's to try to sell his goods to the tavern keeper. Sam Semple fell all over him with joy. The troops swarming into town had caused a serious drain on all supplies but particularly whiskey. He was so eager that Harry drew back. Before he made a final deal, he decided, he would canvass all the taverns in town, in order to get the best possible price. And before the morning was over, he had disposed of salt, whiskey, and Sukey's herbs, and was the proud possessor of a spinning wheel, a grindstone, several kegs for next year's whiskey, ten yards of gray kersey, and a magnificent pair of oxen.

They were rust brown and white, enormous beasts with bulging brown eyes and white horns poked gently forward. MacBain stopped work with a whistle as Harry led them into the smithy. "How you plan to get them upriver?" he said after a minute.

"Afoot. We did it with the handcart our first trip. I can follow the path we made then."

The smith walked around the animals admiringly. "They's right good lookin' beasts, Harry, and that's a fact."

Why was it that a piece of praise from MacBain could make Harry swell up all out of shape? He realized, now that he had Anse's approval, that he would never really have liked or trusted the oxen if Anse hadn't admired them. He shouldn't let the man get such a hold on him.

It took Anse two weeks to sell his property, take out a Virginia deed to the land on the Olethey, and get all his movables packed up. He and Harry fashioned two toboggans, one for each ox, and loaded them up with Anse's goods, Belle's and Maynard's few belongings, Harry's new purchases, and corn and hay for the animals.

Midway through the selling-out process, Lord Dunmore left town, he and his soldiers piling into every available boat and pushing off down the Ohio. Bad luck to the man, thought Harry savagely. I hope a Shawnee arrow finds him.

But it didn't. The fighting took place before he even got there. Word came, the morning Harry and MacBain were packing up their last keg, that the contingent commanded by Andrew Lewis had fought a battle with the Shawnee led by a chief named Cornstalk and won.

"Do you think Showanyaw can have been there?" Harry asked MacBain while they were digesting this latest news.

"More'n likely. Now, lookee here, don't you go frettin' 'bout no Injun. He can take care of hisself."

"I reckon."

"Well, come on then, help me lash down this blamed keg."

At noon the little procession started, with Maynard perched on the rearmost keg, thin brown legs dangling. There was little to be seen of the path Harry had so laboriously cut eighteen months earlier—an occasional stump or log thrown across a brook. They had to chop away as much undergrowth as before and to be as careful of keeping the Allegheny in view. The slow-plodding oxen moved at no faster pace than he had pushing the handcart, too, so that it took three full days to cover the distance.

It was late on their third day of travel that Harry climbed a tree and, peering far and wide, spotted a stump-filled clearing with two cabins. His heart thumped. Home. He had been half afraid again that some stray war party might have come prowling around—or, worse, some party of Virginians. But all seemed to be well. A thin trickle of smoke drifted from the chimney top, and a speck of orange showed where pumpkins were being dried for winter fare.

It was foolish to feel so attached to a mere place. But Harry had given his heart to that little valley, and now it warmed with pleasure at the thought that it was his.

"Come on," he said, climbing down, "we'll just be in time for supper."

Sukey heard the sound of their voices as they struggled to ford the Olethey and came running out of the cabin. At sight of the oxen, her mouth fell open and she pressed her hands to it. Then she came hurrying to meet them. One quick hug for Harry, then she had eyes for nothing but the great rust-colored creatures.

"Oh, Harry, you must have done marvelously!" she cried, arms around the neck of one ox.

"Yes. There were troops from Virginia in town, so prices were high. Mr. Ormsby said he wouldn't have parted with them if he hadn't been desperate."

"We can pull stumps this winter! Oh, Harry, they're beautiful!"

He walked around the animals, slapping flanks, in all pride of possession. Now they could really call themselves farmers.

Sukey did the same, and though she could not have failed to see Belle and Maynard, she pretended not to. Harry allowed her a minute or two to decide what her attitude would be, then he said, "Uh—Sukey, Anse is moving up here permanently."

"Permanently," she echoed blankly. "Oh, hello, Belle. You're a long way from your own fireside."

"So am," the housekeeper burst out wrathfully. She had

grumbled all the way from Pittsburgh, partly from the discomforts of the journey, partly from fear. "Wisht I was back to the Forks, 'stead of comin' all this way through them spooky woods. How I know Injun ain't gone jump out ahind a tree and take he ax to me?"

"You'll get used to the woods," Sukey soothed her. "As for Indians, Pittsburgh has far more of them—and more warlike ones, too—than we do." But she shot a cool look at Anse that seemed reproachful. "But what are we standing here for? Come inside. I'll have supper ready for us in a few minutes."

Harry led the oxen up to the old dugout, which was to be their temporary stable, strewed the floor with some dry leaves, and gave the animals their evening grain. Possessing them gave him an odd thrill, something like the feeling he'd had when he first got his rifle. It was difficult to leave them and go back to the cabin for his meal.

As they ate, MacBain explained how he had bought the acreage next to theirs and meant to build a cabin and forge there and do a bit of farming. "S'posin' you was to come along, Miss Susannah," he added with a bold grin, "and pick out the place where the cabin's to stand?"

Her attitude toward MacBain was certainly strange. She ignored the suggestion and its implications. "That's an odd thing for a master smith to do," she said. "Abandon his trade."

"I like it hereabouts. 'Sides, I ain't abandonin' smithin'. I can do forgin' same as I did these here last months, and take it to the Forks oncet a year. How 'bout the cabin?"

"Don't you think Belle should pick out the site? It's to be her home, apparently."

"Ain't no home of mine," the housekeeper muttered. "All 'lone in the woods."

"I'm hopin' it'll soon have a new mistress."

"Oh?"

"That there ain't no news to you, Miss Susannah. You come pick out a place for me."

She hesitated, and Harry saw her lips tremble very slightly. But she had her voice under control: "I think not. There's a reason."

"You don't like slavery," MacBain stated bluntly. "I know. But I'm agoin' to court you anyways."

Sukey whirled on Harry. "You *told* him!"

"I had to. Good lack, Sukey, I couldn't let the man sell up his shop and buy land up here without knowing exactly what his chances were. Of course, I told him."

"And I thought 'bout it a powerful long time, and I decided." He looked Sukey clear in the face. "I ain't givin' them their freedom, not just for to please a woman. And I'm still agoin' to come courtin'."

It was the old self-confident MacBain. Harry glanced curiously from him to his sister. How would she take that? She sat without speaking, but that didn't mean she had been silenced—not Sukey.

"And right here, in front of your brother," MacBain surged on, "I'm askin' you proper: Will you marry me, Susannah Warrilow?"

Sukey said levelly, "No," and got up from the table and left the cabin.

15

Troubles Mount Up

Sukey wasn't one to sulk or bang pots or play martyr, but it was obvious in the next weeks that she was drenched in unhappiness. Harry watched helplessly and once or twice tried to make her accept the fact of slavery, but he was always hastily silenced. She spent a lot of time using her new spinning wheel.

The trouble was that Harry could understand how both sides felt. However much a man loves a woman, he's a fool if he lets her run his life. MacBain seemed to think that if he gave in on this matter of Belle and Maynard, he'd soon be giving in on everything. And Sukey—well, Harry didn't share her passionate hatred for slavery, but he could see how, having it, she couldn't bring herself to marry a man who held slaves.

So, a strain.

They were most desperately busy that fall, too. In the end it was Harry who picked out a site for the MacBain cabin—halfway up the side of a hill overlooking the Allegheny. Then while MacBain felled timbers, Harry squared and notched them, and Belle and Maynard collected rocks for the forge and chimney. They built a big cabin, twice the size of Harry's, with two rooms downstairs and the forge and cooking hearth in the middle, sharing a common chimney. The smith and his two servants moved in in mid-November, and his old cabin became Harry's stable. As a precaution, Harry cut a window in the back of his own cabin—no more having to knock off a shingle. Then it was time to tackle the stumps.

Christmas came and went, and then it was 1775. Harry was determined to have at least one acre of ground plowable by spring. So every morning he set out with his ax and Tip and Terry, the oxen, and labored over stumps. Sometimes he could get out two a day. Other times, he'd find himself struggling for a week over one. But little by little they came out and were burned, and by May planting time, he had his acre cleared.

But he was never to get it plowed. For that week disaster struck.

Sukey fell ill suddenly. She was cranky and irritable all one day, complaining of a pain in her side. Then that evening she began to vomit and turned feverish, and the following morning she was unable to get out of bed.

"I'm sorry, Harry," she groaned. "You'll have to get your own breakfast."

"Don't worry about me. Get some rest." He went out to feed the oxen and muck out the stable and then returned to stand over his sister anxiously. "Anything I can get you?"

"Ohhhh," she said and then lay as if too exhausted to say more. Finally she roused up a trifle. "Perhaps some pennyroyal tea."

He searched through the bark containers in which she kept her simples, sniffing their strong and various aromas. He wasn't at all sure he could pick out pennyroyal. "Is this the pennyroyal?" he asked her, holding out what seemed the likeliest candidate.

"What? Oh, yes, that's it."

He put a pinch of dried leaf in a cup and added hot water from a kettle on the fire. "Here's your tea. Shall I hold the cup while you drink?"

She stared at him blankly.

"I—I reckon I'd best help you." He set the tea down on a stool, slid an arm behind Sukey's shoulders, and lifted her partway up. Good God, her body felt hot! Her head lolled against his shoulder, and he could see that it was damp with perspiration. "Here now, try and drink a bit," Harry said, bringing the cup to her lips.

She did sip a little, and her throat worked. But she'd taken in no more than a quarter of the cup when her body heaved, and tea and stomach fluid flowed out over the bedclothes. "Sorry . . ." she whispered. "Sorry . . ."

Harry cleaned up the mess, then stood looking down at the sick girl. He was beginning to be frightened.

This wasn't a little catarrh, a little passing ague. Sukey was really ill. She had began to breathe rapidly, almost panting, and was seized with a fit of coughing that left her limp as a rag.

He shook his head. He had to get help. No doctor, of course, but someone who could do nursing. Would Belle be willing? Women knew about these things. Yes, if it got any worse, he'd fetch Belle.

"Harry," Sukey moaned, "get a cold cloth, please. My head is splitting."

Good notion—a cold cloth would help the fever, too.

Harry hunted around the cabin. During the winter, Sukey had turned the ten yards of kersey into a jacket and breeches for him and a dress for herself. There were pieces of it left over. He ripped off a good-sized swatch, then brought in a bucket of water and dipped in the cloth. He pressed this to Sukey's face—forehead, left cheek, right cheek, under the chin, around the back of the neck, then the forehead again. She made little response.

Over and over he worked, drawing fresh cold water as the old warmed up. Sukey seemed in a kind of stupor, neither wholly conscious nor wholly in a coma. From time to time she had a fit of coughing. In between, there was only that quick, shallow breathing broken by a weary groan.

Outside it began to rain, and every tree drip-dripped. Well, Harry consoled himself, he couldn't plow today anyway.

Sometimes Sukey would rouse up and appear almost lucid—"Harry, don't go away. Hold my hand, Harry"—but in a moment or two, back she'd slip into half-consciousness again. By nightfall she was beginning to mutter with delirium, head rolling from side to side on the cornhusk pillow. Harry did not dare go to the loft that night. He put fresh logs on the fire, fried himself a bit of johnnycake, and sat down again at the bedside.

From time to time, he dozed off, to pull himself up with a jerk a few minutes later. Sukey was always much the same. Finally, knowing that his ministrations were doing little to help, he stretched out at the side of the bed and let himself go fully asleep. No good both of them being ill.

He woke at dawn, stirred up the fire, and bent over Sukey. She went into one of her coughing spasms, and this time, Harry noted with a gasp, it left ominous spots of red on the quilt.

This would not do. He had to get help.

"Sukey," he said as though she still could hear and reply, "I'm going for Belle. I'll be back—oh, in an hour." One last time he rinsed out the cold cloth and laid it over her forehead. Then he caught up his jacket and rifle, pulled his battered old tricorne hat well down on his forehead, and set out for MacBain's.

They had visited back and forth two or three times a week during the winter, so there was a well-worn path. It was still raining. Harry slogged along as fast as he could through the mud and the dripping trees. Ah, a glimpse of the Allegheny, and here was the clearing, with its double cabin. Smoke poured from the chimney. The latch string was out. Harry pulled it and burst in.

"Anse," he said breathlessly, "it's Sukey. She's sick—bad sick. Can Belle come?"

The smith had just unbanked his forge fire. The roused embers cast a pink glow over the startled face he turned to Harry. "Sick? Miss Susannah?"

"Yes. It's lung fever, I think. Anyway something wrong with her breathing. She's—out of her head a lot. I thought—well, a woman would know better than I do. Anse, I'm scared."

MacBain moved swiftly to rebank the fire, calling, "Belle! Get your shawl, take Maynard, and come. Miss Susannah needs us."

It was a relief to have someone else to share the problem, especially Anse who acted, crisply and efficiently, instead of asking a lot of questions or bemoaning the difficulty. Already Harry felt better. If there was a way to get Sukey well, Anse would think of it.

Belle now, she was a bemoaner. "Oh, me, I surely do feel bad with Miss Sukey sick. All 'lone in that there cabin with Mist' Harry. Away off up here in the woods, ain't no doctor, ain't no nothing. Oh, me, oh, me . . ."

It was Maynard who first spotted the disaster.

He'd been dancing on ahead. The mud did not impede his light heels with any success. He made a game of swishing it from side to side, running off to clear patches to make fresh footprints, yelling, "Whooo-eeee!" Once he got so far ahead that he disappeared from view. When they saw him again, his air had quite changed. He came creeping back to them, puzzled and fearful.

"Who them?" he said to Harry.

Harry's heart skipped a beat. "Them?"

"All them men with horses."

"What men?"

"All *them* men." And, horribly, Harry guessed.

He and Anse looked at one another. "Girty," said Anse. "Wager anythin' you own."

"Not taken."

With one accord, they began to run. Oh, no, oh, no, Harry thought. Sukey alone and ill, and that animal in possession. Suppose—? No, Girty was greedy, that's all. He wouldn't harm her. Would he? No, no, of course he wouldn't. . . .

They saw the group before they themselves emerged from the woods. Instinctively both Anse and Harry got behind trees, and Anse motioned Belle to do the same. There were a number of men milling about in the clearing, dressed like any frontiersmen—some fetching sticks for a fire, some exploring the stable cabin or wandering boldly in and out of the house cabin, others holding horses or just leaning on their rifles. Simon Girty was not in sight, and for a moment Harry let himself feel encouraged. Maybe they were just a party of traders, heading for Kittanning. But, no, only one of the horses carried a pack saddle. Harry counted them.

"Eleven horses—one with pack saddle," he said to Anse, low. "That probably means ten men in all. And look—that's Girty coming out of the cabin now."

"You say Miss Susannah's in there, with all them men marchin' in and out?"

"Yes, curse it." Harry wanted to grab his rifle and run pellmell across the clearing and put a ball square in that raffish black head. But common sense told him the patient way was the only one that had a chance of working. Girty had caught them unprepared and seized their property. Now they had to think of some way to run him off.

"Hey, Drummond!" they heard the distant Girty shout. "Sanderson! Frazer!" He finished with a come-here jerk of the head, and three of the men left what they were doing and gathered around him at the cabin door. At the end of a few minutes' confab, the three broke away and began to cast about the clearing as though hunting for something. They found Harry's fresh tracks without trouble and began to follow them.

"Hunting for me," Harry said. "Keep hidden until they're past us, then try to take them prisoner."

MacBain nodded grimly.

The three men entered the woods, approached the place where Harry and the others lay in ambush and were just noticing that up ahead were the tracks of more than one person when Harry stepped out, rifle leveled.

"Drop those rifles," he said. From the other side of the path, MacBain had emerged too.

The men swung around, faces blank with surprise. One of them opened his mouth to yell to Girty, but Harry saw him drawing his breath for the effort and jabbed him in the throat with the rifle butt. He dropped his rifle and sprawled in the mud, where he lay for a minute, swallowing hard and rubbing his bruised Adam's apple.

"Drop those rifles," Harry said again to the other men. "And keep your mouths shut."

When they had sullenly obeyed, Harry gestured to the wide-eyed Maynard. "Run back to Mister Anse's cabin and fetch a good long piece of rope. Hurry now."

The boy gave a shrill "Whooo-eeee!" and danced off, delighted at the exciting things that were happening. His mother, who was huddled behind her tree, almost visibly shaking, plainly did not derive any pleasure from the proceedings at all.

"Belle, can you carry three rifles?"

"Oh, Mist' Harry, I don't want touch one of them things. I scairt of them."

"There's nothing to be afraid of."

"I a housekeeper, not a soldier man, Mist' Harry. Don't ax me to carry no gun."

"Belle," said MacBain in a here-we-go-again voice, "pick up them rifles. You can see Harry and I has to keep ourn at the ready."

Reluctant and grumbling, Belle collected the rifles of

their prisoners. The man who had been hit in the throat was back on his feet by now. The three men were watchful and hostile, but Harry didn't think they would risk anything much for Girty's sake. With the rifle, he gestured up the path, and the men turned around and sulkily marched off.

Halfway to MacBain's they met Maynard, returning with an immense festoon of rope draped about his slender person. The party stopped long enough to tie the prisoners' hands behind their backs. Harry then felt secure enough to relieve Belle of the captured rifles and securer still when they reached the smithy and bound the men hand and foot.

They questioned the men, but there was little to be learned that they did not know or had guessed. Girty had won over a new set of men with promises of wealth to be had from salt boiling, and here they were. They had caught Harry off guard and were in possession.

"That there sister of yourn, she don't seem to be seein' the future so good this time," one of them snickered. He had been among the first party.

"No, she's sick."

"Yep, we seen."

But they looked uneasy at this reminder, and that inspired Harry to tell a lie: "We think it's smallpox."

Dismay flooded their rugged faces. *"Smallpox!"* the three of them chorused. Then one thought twice. "She ain't got no smallpox. I seen her. No rash."

"Rash doesn't come on right away. Does it, Anse?"

"Sure don't. Y'all are goin' to be mighty sick boys in a few days. Specially them as spends aplenty of time in that there cabin."

They looked more and more uneasy, but one tried to

shake off his fear with bluster: "We are, hey? And what about *him*? He been with her for days, more'n likely."

"I was inoculated in the Army," Harry said, which, as a matter of fact, was true.

"In the Army? What army? Not the Regulars?"

"That's right. Twenty-ninth Foot."

The one who had blustered now seemed for a moment to forget his predicament. "You served in the Regulars? Say, lookee here, my company's been tryin' to find us a good drill sergeant for a long time. And what with the news from Boston and all, mebbe you'd have the mind to—"

"Good lack!" Harry cried, outraged. "You come up here to rob me of my land and push my poor sister out of her own sickbed, and on top of it you have the gall to try to recruit me for your foul militia!"

The man subsided as though it had occurred to him, too, that this was not the time and place for an enlistment speech. And in the short silence that followed, Harry belatedly heard the other thing the man had said.

"What news from Boston?"

"What *news*? Oh, I reckon, livin' way up here, you ain't heard yet."

"Heard what?"

"Why, man, the Regulars. They went marchin' out of Boston last month to grab up some militia stores at a town called Concord, and them Yankee soldiers attacked and druv them all the way back to town. It's war now, they say."

There was a burst of excited gossip between MacBain and the prisoner, but Harry digested this stunning news in silence. He didn't believe it for a moment. Not the way the man told it. Massachusetts rabble set Regulars to running? Not bloody likely. But they had apparently *attacked* them.

He felt a kind of glow spread through him. Someone had finally done something. Someone had finally had too much of tyrannical jackanapes in office and had put in a blow for home rule. He wished he'd been there. It wouldn't have been easy for him, who used to wear one, to draw a bead on a red coat, but he wished he'd been there all the same.

But he couldn't stand here like this, woolgathering about some incident five hundred miles away. There was Sukey to rescue. Harry had begun to worry desperately about her. He'd been gone two hours now, and in the meantime there were those men traipsing in and out— why, cold air and drafts alone could do untold damage.

And yet what could he do?

MacBain abandoned gossip and voiced the same question: "Well, what now, Harry?"

"Go back there. Set another ambush. Look the ground over. Try to think of something."

So, leaving Belle with orders to see that the men didn't get free of their bonds, they set off through the forest for Harry's clearing.

Things had livened up some, they could see as they crouched in the lee of a fallen log and looked out. The bonfire was roaring furiously now, and the men were setting up a crude cooking rack. Two of them emerged from the stable carrying what looked like a side of beef—a side of something, anyway. Harry, his jaw dropping, caught sight of a bloody hide on the ground.

For a moment his mind refused to register what it meant. Then he leaped to his feet, caution forgotten.

"They've killed Tip," he said in a voice even he did not recognize. "They've killed Tip. For *food.*"

"Hush now," MacBain soothed him. "Ain't doin' no good givin' ourselves away."

"But—but they've murdered a first-class draft animal! To *eat* him! They're all woodsmen. Game is everywhere. And they had to kill a trained farm animal!"

"Them no 'counts do things like that—no sense to them 'tall. Now get aholt of yourself. Think of Miss Susannah."

"But—but—but—" Harry was so outraged that he could only sputter uselessly. Wildly he debated rushing out on the men like the Yankees at—what was its name?— Concord, and shooting them down in their tracks. He felt murderous. He had never hated anyone so savagely in his life. "They might as well take Terry, too," he raged on when he found his tongue again. "Oxen don't take to new partners. Kill one, might as well kill the other. All that money, dragging them all the way from Pittsburgh, and now these—these pirates just up and make a meal of them."

But at last he let MacBain pull him back down into hiding. Not that his anger had abated one trifle. He hadn't felt indignant over his sister's fate—he had been too frightened to be angry—and now rage worked to stimulate his mind. Plans and schemes fairly flew through his head, were debated, considered, discarded, replaced all in an instant.

Stop up the chimney, smoke them out? Not with Sukey in there, already sick in the lungs.

Rush in on them, seize one as prisoner? What good would one do? And you couldn't repeat the trick because they'd be on their guard.

Wait till dark, then advance on the cabin? That hadn't

worked for Girty, and there was no reason to think he hadn't learned from his own failure.

Wait here in ambush as originally planned, try to take more captives? Too uncertain. And too tame—far too tame for the rage that burned in Harry.

Try to make them think there were more men here than just Harry and MacBain? Harry paused longer over this idea. They had five rifles between them. Suppose they could rig them up in some fashion, so that they pointed toward the cabin from different points in the woods and fixed so they could be fired from here?

No, it wouldn't work. Girty's party was still seven in number, same as the first group. They wouldn't be scared off by five men, especially since they had possession of the cabin.

And of Sukey. Oh, God, what was happening to her? Was she even still alive? They'd come through so much together, it didn't seem possible that their dreams could now be hovering on the brink of death. But she was ill—terribly, dangerously ill. And alone in a crowd of rowdy enemies. He had to get her out. He had to think of a way.

Why not just walk in peacefully and take her? Why should Girty want to keep him from carrying away a sick person? Harry stood up. "Anse, cover me just in case."

"What you fixin' to do?"

"Get Sukey out. That's got to come before anything else."

"You're right," MacBain said grimly. "Take her to my place. Where," he added under his breath, "she belongs."

16
Saving Sukey

Harry braced himself and slipped out into the path, heading resolutely toward the clearing. He kept his gaze fixed on the cabin as he stepped out into the open, but he was aware of the men's startled reaction: an exclamation from someone, another whipping about in surprise, a third rising from a crouch, one body after another stopping what it was doing and turning to stare.

He carefully ignored the butchered ox, still fixing his eyes on the house. The bonfire was directly in front of the cabin door, so he had to go quite close to Girty and his men, but he said nothing and would have passed on without acknowledging their presence if Girty himself had not stepped into his path.

"Well, greenhorn, here we are again. Thought you'd druv us away for good, hey?"

"You're ahead for the moment," Harry acknowledged coolly, "but not for long. I've come for my sister."

Girty produced a wolfish smile. "That there girl is aplenty sick iffen you was to ax me."

"Yes, smallpox."

"Small—?" He gulped, the grin vanishing, and from the others came a disturbed sound.

"We expect the rash to break out any time now," Harry went on, to forestall any inconvenient questions. "I can handle her, you see, because I've got the protection."

He stepped around Girty and went inside.

He was half afraid to take a close look at Sukey, but when he did, he saw she was much as before—coughing, stuporous, panting for breath. As he bent over her, she roused up a little. "Harry, there were some men—"

"I know, Sukey, I know. Now I'm going to have to move you. We'll go to MacBain's. I'll be as easy as I can, but—well, it won't be comfortable."

For answer, she groaned weakly.

He went outside, whipped past the men—now muttering together and rolling their eyes, superstitiously—and into the stable. Poor Terry lowed dismally, and Harry paused to give him a distracted pat before unearthing one of the toboggans they had used for the last journey from Pittsburgh. He toyed with the idea of taking Terry, too, but Girty might object, and the chief thing now was to rescue Sukey and get out quickly. He dragged the toboggan to the cabin and inside.

He laid out their one bearskin as a mattress, wrapped all the quilts they owned around Sukey, then lifted her and laid her on the toboggan, with her cornhusk pillow under her head. He took her precious collection of herbs along as well, in case she was ever able to hold any medicine down.

The men were still standing around when he drew the toboggan through the cabin door. He was half convinced they meant to attack him and eyed them warily as he came abreast. But far from trying to stop him, they all pulled hastily away to give him a wide berth.

Walking as quickly as he could without jarring the toboggan, Harry crossed the clearing and entered the path. When he reached a point well screened from the cabin, MacBain popped out of hiding. The smith bent over the toboggan.

"Sukey? Sukey?" he said in consternation. It was the first time Harry could remember the man using her nickname. "Gorries, Harry, she *is* right bad."

"Yes, let's hurry and get her to your place. It would be easier on her if we carried the toboggan. Can you take the front end?"

Between them they transported the sick girl the mile or so to MacBain's cabin and installed her in Belle's bed, where Belle herself took over the nursing.

That done, Harry gave himself a mental shake. He could do nothing more for his sister at the moment—it was up to God and nature to decide her fate. What he had to do now was concentrate on getting rid of Girty and his men.

With MacBain trotting at his heels, he jogged back toward his own clearing. One by one he reviewed the ideas he had had earlier, and, as before, reluctantly discarded them as still unworkable. But then he remembered one of them—stopping the chimney. Now that Sukey was out of the cabin, that one *was* workable. Suppose they smoked the men out and seized them as they emerged?

He mulled the idea over for a few minutes and could find no loopholes in it. In growing excitement he put it to MacBain.

"Smoke them out?" the smith mused, a grin slowly

stealing over his face. "That there's a first-rate idee, Harry. Have to wait for nightfall, though."

"Wait?" Harry echoed disappointedly, but as soon as he'd said it, he realized MacBain was right. They were too weak to be bold. Stealth was their only weapon. "Right. Now what do we need?"

MacBain had automatically taken some rope along this time, and the only other equipment they needed was a ladder. They spent the afternoon finding a young tree, cutting it down, and notching it at intervals for "rungs." They made one anxious visit to MacBain's cabin and found things there unchanged. Then as darkness fell over the forest, they silently returned to their hiding place and peered out at Harry's clearing.

The bonfire was down to a mere glow, and a heap of bones and half-gnawed joints marked the site of the celebration banquet. No one was in sight. Harry wondered if they had found the keg of whiskey he always kept back from a season's distilling for home purposes. He hoped they had. A cabinful of drunks would be a lot easier to handle than a cabinful of the sober and the alert.

"They's sleepin' in the stable," MacBain pointed out. Sure enough, the slenderest finger of smoke was rising from the second cabin, none from Harry's own.

"Not taking any chances of smallpox," Harry said with a grim smile. It was good to know that they had made that much impression on the invaders. "Come on."

Slipping from tree to tree, they moved as close as they could to the stable without crossing open ground. They had to assume that Girty had been cautious enough to post a watch. At last, though, it came time to leave shelter and advance boldly to the side of the cabin.

There the two huddled, ears pressed against the log

walls. A voice muttered. Awake? Or only dreaming drunkenly? Crouching, Harry slipped around to the front of the building where the only window was. A crack in the shutter showed a streak of red—presumably the banked cabin fire. From the wood stack that leaned against the stable wall, Harry took a couple of chunks—one to feed the fire, the others to block the chimney.

He jerked his head at MacBain, and together they got the ladder into position. Harry went up it, moving as quietly as he could, and straddled the ridgepole, from which seat he peered down into the depths of the chimney. There was a fire all right. Taking a deep breath, he slid one bit of firewood into the chimney and watched it drop down and land in a shower of sparks. Then quickly he laid the other pieces of wood across the mouth of the chimney.

If the men inside weren't awakened by the noise, they soon would be by the smoke. Harry crawled down the roof to a position directly above the cabin door. MacBain remained around to the side, holding both their rifles. They waited.

Inside, someone coughed. Smoke seeped out from around the edges of the shutter, of the cabin door, through an unchinked place along the caves. Another cough, a bewildered mutter: "Whuzzamatter? Whuzzall that there smoke?"

They *are* drunk! Harry exulted.

Then came a growl from Girty: "Smoke? Somethin' wrong with the chimney? That no 'count greenhorn is up to his tricks, I'll be bound. Dan, go look."

Dan objected sleepily, but after a bit of swearing and a lot of coughing, he dragged himself to the door. Harry poised to jump. The door opened a crack, and for a

moment nothing happened. Girty's men weren't so drunk
as not to take precautions. Then a tousle-headed figure
appeared, a rifle on its arm, and peered around in every
direction. In every direction except up.

Harry leaped. He landed on Dan's shoulders, carrying
him forward onto the ground, where his cries of surprise
were muffled in the mud. The rifle went off, and the
recoil left Dan with what appeared to be a numb and
momentarily useless arm.

The cabin door slammed shut, and rifle muzzles
appeared at the window, but Harry had his prisoner. He
whipped him up as a shield fast enough to prevent the
men at the window from firing. He didn't even need
MacBain, who rushed to his support with a rifle in either

hand, to help him jerk Dan to his feet and around the side of the cabin, where they trussed him up good and proper.

Now what?

They had lost the element of surprise. Girty's men wouldn't venture out now—not in ones or twos anyway. Harry had hoped to capture at least two men this way, reduce Girty's party to a mere five.

They heard thumps and bangs centering on the chimney. Apparently Girty's men were trying to dislodge the blocking chunks of wood from inside. Then, *Crk-ooooom!*

The chimney-stopping firewood sailed sky high, impelled by a blast from a rifle. Harry and MacBain ducked the descending fragments, and Harry immediately climbed the ladder with more firewood. That, too, was shot away, and so was the third set.

Harry looked down at MacBain from his perch. "Keep this up and run them out of powder?"

MacBain shrugged. "They's ten of them. Take you a week to run them all out of powder."

But he handed up more firewood, and Harry blocked the chimney for the fourth time. Another *crk-ooooom!* sent it flying too. Well, Harry thought, at least we're getting that chimney well swept. He laid a fifth set of blocks across the chimney mouth.

As he did, he heard something. A faint something-—something so soft it was almost felt rather than heard. Someone was in the loft. They were going to try on him the trick he had played on them!

Hastily Harry shifted from rooftree to ladder and whispered, "Anse, my rifle." With the weapon in hand, he held it pointed along the line of shakes, ready to swing in any direction.

Thump! There they were. They hadn't got the shake off in one blow the way Harry had. He sighted his rifle on the spot, and as a second *thump!* flung up the shake, he fired at the flinging arm.

"Dad-blast the plaguy—!"

Whoever had been about to fire through the loosened shake retired swiftly in a storm of swear words. Inside, angry voices rose. Evidently Girty's men had again not counted on being wounded and didn't like it. Good. If he had to, Harry would wound them all, one by one.

Girty managed to silence this first outburst, for the voices soon fell silent. Another *crk-ooooom!* disposed of the fifth set of chimney blockers. Before he laid on a sixth, Harry peered down the chimney. A face was peering up at him.

"Girty?" he said, recognizing it.

"Yep, greenhorn."

"We can keep this up until you run out of powder."

"We got plenty of powder."

"Have you got plenty of men, too? Because we have four of them prisoner now and mean to capture the rest at our leisure. Or shoot them," he added carelessly.

"Iffen you live that long. I'm gittin' plenty sick of you, boy."

"I'm not letting you have this property, Girty. Whatever I have to do to keep it, I'll do."

Another voice spoke from inside the cabin: "Whyn't you and him fight it out atween you?"

There was an enthusiastic chorus of agreement. Girty's men would far rather see the principals in an all-out scrap than have to bear the brunt of it themselves. Harry could hardly blame them.

"We're finished here tonight," he said. He had come to

a sudden decision. "Tomorrow we're going to Kittanning for help. Then we'll be back to run you out."

They returned to MacBain's cabin with their prisoner, leading Terry. "You mean that 'bout goin' to Kittannin'?" MacBain inquired dubiously.

"No, but I want Girty to think I have a way of getting extra backers. We have six rifles now, and there ought to be a way to set them up to look like six men. I don't reckon Girty's people are the sort to stand up to equal numbers."

But plans for getting rid of Girty were pushed aside when they reached MacBain's, for Sukey's illness was approaching some kind of crisis.

"Thank God you come, Mist' Anse!" Belle cried as they entered the cabin. "She so sick, I don't know what to do."

Heart in his mouth, Harry approached the bed. Sukey did look worse—chest heaving, eyes vacant and rolling, flesh burning hot. " 'Bout a hour ago, she come on bad," the poor housekeeper said. "Nothin' I done helped any, Mist' Anse, and I scairt she like to die."

"Harry . . . Harry . . ." she moaned faintly, "some men . . . some men came. . . ."

"Don't try to talk. We know about the men. It's all right, Belle, I'll take over."

Anse fetched a fresh bucket of cold water and wrung out a cloth, and Harry began his ministrations—cold cloth to Sukey's forehead, cheeks, throat, over and over again. She was drenched in perspiration, her breathing shallow. Harry had some notion that she could breathe better if she were raised up, so he pulled her up against him and rested her head on his shoulder. Then forehead . . . cheeks . . . throat . . .

MacBain didn't say much, just sat on a stool on the far

side of the bed and watched. It pained Harry to look at his face. If Sukey weren't so stubborn—or Anse either, for that matter—he would have had the right to nurse her now, instead of looking on helplessly.

Harry was so tired he thought his arms would drop off. He had had little sleep last night, and after a day of alarums a second night without sleep was beginning to tell on him. Oh, Sukey, Sukey, don't die! We haven't come all this way together for you to die on me! Forehead . . . cheeks . . . throat . . . forehead . . . cheeks . . . throat . . .

They sent Belle to get what sleep she could on the floor before the fire. Harry longed to join her, but tired as he was, he didn't think he could sleep with Sukey like this. Forehead . . . cheeks . . . throat . . . On and on, hour after hour. Forehead . . . cheeks . . . throat . . .

Gradually it was borne in on Harry that Sukey was breathing more easily. And she had not coughed in—oh, at least an hour. He paused to lay a cheek against hers. Surely it was less warm now than it had been. She drew a long sigh, and the tension slipped from her struggling body. Harry lowered her to the pillow and drew up the quilt.

He tapped MacBain, who had dozed off, on the knee. "What do you think?" he whispered as the smith lumbered to his feet. "It looks to me like a good sleep."

MacBain took a limp hand and held it lightly. "She's better," he whispered. "You go git you some sleep. I'll watch now."

Gratefully Harry sprawled on the floor by the fire, across from Belle, and plunged headlong into sleep. Time enough to worry about Girty tomorrow.

17
Battle Royal

It was nearly noon before Harry woke. Even Belle's cooking, carried on over and around him, had not disturbed his heavy slumbers, nor yet the sound of MacBain at work at his anvil or the prisoners cursing one another in the smithy where they were tied up. But he felt fine as he got to his feet and went to see how Sukey was.

Her face had the wasted, lined look of someone recently ill, and she was so weak she could barely lift a hand to him, but she was herself again and managed a smile.

"Feeling better?" he asked, oddly shy.

"Much, thanks to you, Harry. Anse said you were the one who brought me through."

"Well, it had to be me, didn't it? You don't have a husband." Now why had he said that? He had wounded her—it showed on her face. "I'm—I'm sorry, Sukey. But last night—I reckon Anse would have given anything for the right to be the one to tend you."

She turned her head away, and seeing it was no use pleading Anse's cause, he went on into the smithy part of the cabin. "Are you coming to help me rig up the rifles?"

"Yep. But it don't make no sense to do the thing in daylight. After dark. 'Sides, we'll need plenty of these here." He held up an eyed spike which he was busy forging.

"I reckon you're right." But Harry sighed restlessly. He wanted to *do* something. His glance fell on the sullen prisoners, bearded and dirty and rope-burned at wrist and ankle. Suddenly struck, he said, "Anse, why hasn't Girty done anything about these men?"

"Don't know. Mebbe he has."

"You mean—?" Harry glanced over his shoulder as though the burly Mr. Girty were creeping up behind. Then, sheepishly, he said, "Maybe he's waiting for darkness, too."

"Si will get us out of this here," one of the prisoners said boldly, but the others did not back him up. They just looked at one another as though hoping for reassurance and not finding it.

Harry ate the mush Belle had prepared for him, then went out to explore the lay of the land. When he got to his own clearing, he found it deserted. Moving cautiously, he peered into the stable. It smelled a bit of dirty human beings, and there were a few heaps of strange belongings, but no one to be seen. The cabin contained five horses. Obviously the six men had gone somewhere on horseback. To the salt spring? That was why they were here, wasn't it?

Harry set off for the spring, circling around through the woods so as to come on it from above. And sure enough, there they were. They had taken over Harry's kettle and were busily chopping wood to feed the fire that burned under it.

I could shoot Girty dead and end it all, he thought vengefully. But it would be his own end, too, if he did.

Girty's men would be on him long before he could reload.

Then he was distracted by thought of the kettle.

Just how far did Girty's aggression go? he wondered. Obviously he considered the land rightfully his by virtue of his Virginia deed. But did the land include Harry's and Sukey's movable belongings as well? He rather suspected not. At least Girty might try to make such a claim, but his followers—rough and crude as they were, frontiersmen had strong ideas about property—his followers probably would not allow it. Well, he'd let the kettle go for the time being.

He faded back into the woods, returned to MacBain's cabin, and spent the rest of the day chopping firewood. Belle was going to launder the next day and would need a lot of hot water.

After dark, armed with the six rifles, a dozen eyed spikes that MacBain had made, and plenty of rope, they set off for Harry's cabin. All was dark and still in the clearing. Moving quietly, they slipped around to the far side and chose positions for the four captured rifles and lashed them to suitable trees. They were loaded with powder only. The triggers were looped with fine cord, which ran down to one of the eyed spikes, through that and on to tie up with a heavier grade of rope. The rope was then threaded through another spike on another tree.

Harry ended up on the opposite side of the clearing with four ropes in his hand, each one crudely controlling the firing of one rifle. He and MacBain shotted their own weapons and took up a position in front of the cabin but hidden by the trees.

Harry cupped his hands around his mouth. "Girty!" he yelled. "We've got you surrounded."

No response.

"Girty!"

"Mebbe we'd best wait till mornin'," MacBain suggested. "They got to come out then."

"No, I've done enough waiting."

Twice more Harry hailed the cabin without getting any reaction. He strode toward it, full of grim and desperate feelings. Their notched-log ladder was lying right where they'd left it, and over against the house was the heap of rocks Harry had been collecting to build a stone chimney. He had an idea. He was going to close the chimney again—and this time not with some easily shot away piece of wood.

He selected the biggest stone in the pile. It wasn't easy just to lift it, and it took him five puffing minutes to haul it up to the roof. But once in place over the chimney top, it formed a solid cap.

"Shoot a rifle at this, Simon Girty, and you won't dislodge it—you'll get a ricochet."

Climbing down, he retired to his original position to await events.

First, smoke seeped out from cracks as it had other times, then angry voices were heard, then a rifle roared—followed by more angry voices. Harry grinned in spite of himself, and MacBain said, "By gorries, I hope it nicked one of them!"

A long wait ensued, punctuated by much coughing. Then the dark rectangle that was the cabin door grew darker along one side. Someone had opened it a crack.

Harry pulled one of his ropes, firing a gun from the far side of the clearing. The door was hastily shut.

"Girty!" Harry yelled. "There are six of us here. We've got you surrounded."

Still no response. But Harry thought he detected an increase in coughing. The place must be filled with smoke. There, the window shutter was opening. That would doubtless help some, but the stable had no rear window, like the cabin, so there was no cross ventilation. Girty could always put out the fire, of course, but dosing a fire up here in the wilderness was not something you undertook lightly.

There was another wait. Then the cabin door opened again. Harry held his fire. A burly figure slipped out, dropped down, and began to crawl toward the chimney. Girty himself. Harry could guess at the quarrel that had forced him to do his own dirty work. He pulled another rope and was delighted to see the man flatten out in the slush.

Girty had his rifle with him as always. He jerked it up and sighted along it from the prone position. Harry

thought he might as well give him something to aim at. He pulled another rope. Girty instantly fired in the direction of the gunfire.

Gleefully Harry leaped out into the clearing, rifle to his shoulder. "Hands up, Girty!"

Caught with an unloaded rifle out in the open, Girty froze. Harry loped across the clearing, keeping his rifle in firing position. "Up!" he said, jerking it. "To your feet."

Gloweringly Girty rose, and the two enemies stood face to face. Armed or not, Harry was careful to stay out of reach of Girty's powerful arm. "That knife at your belt—pull it out and throw it away. The tomahawk, too. All right," he went on when the weapons had been discarded, "straight ahead. March."

It seemed almost too easy. When he reached the place where MacBain was hiding, he held both rifles while the smith tied Girty's hands. Then they settled back to see if they could lure any others out.

But their luck was out, for the next man to emerge could not be startled into firing at something he couldn't see. They had to sit and watch him remove the stone, then dart back inside.

Harry went around reloading the four captured rifles—five now, for they'd taken Girty's too—then climbed up the ladder to replace the stone. When he got back, Girty, who of course had caught on that they had no six men, was cursing freely. "Iffen I could jest git my hands on you, boy," he snarled at Harry, "I'd teach you some powerful good lessons."

Harry did not answer. The cabin door was opening again.

But the men had evidently learned a good lesson of their own, for two of them came out together, and one covered the other while he climbed the ladder. Well, this scheme had obviously run its course.

They collected the rifles and returned to MacBain's cabin with their fifth—and most important—prisoner.

There was a tremendous clamor among their prisoners when they saw Girty. They plainly blamed him for their present plight, for there was a good deal of yelling and cursing and name calling, until MacBain boxed a couple of ears and told them to be quiet for Miss Susannah's sake.

Early the next morning, Harry went to the salt spring and rescued his big kettle. He crouched in the woods awhile, but the men did not show up. What would they do, now they were leaderless? Try to rescue their comrades? Would they feel bound to continue supporting Girty's cause? Obviously they did not feel up to boiling out more salt. What should he and MacBain do now? He could think of more ways to outsmart the men who held Their Place captive. Would a parlay help? Could they be *persuaded* to go away?

Back at MacBain's cabin, Harry turned the kettle over to Maynard whose job it was to heat wash water for his mother over an outdoor fire.

"Well, Anse," Harry said in the smithy, "what now?"

MacBain surveyed the dirty, disheveled prisoners, sitting side by side along the smithy wall, and smiled grimly. "Ain't nothin' we can do 'cept wait them out. What say, Si? How long afore they gits tired of sitting there?"

"We could end all this in a hour," Girty howled, "iffen greenhorn wasn't such of a coward."

"What you mean by that there?"

"Iffen he was willin' to fight me, that'd settle it permanent."

"Harry wasn't raised to your kind of fighting."

"He wasn't raised to no kind of fighting."

"Harry ain't no coward."

"Hold on," Harry said, stepping forward. "When you said 'end this,' did you mean really? Permanently?"

"I sure did."

"You'll surrender your Virginia deed and go away and not try to claim our property again?"

"That's right, greenhorn."

"You'll call off the men still back there in the cabin and these here as well."

"Yep."

Harry looked at MacBain. "Don't do it!" the smith said violently. "You ain't a match for him."

Harry looked back at Girty, once again assessing his chances with the burly man. He was slightly taller but fifty pounds lighter. He would be cruelly punished, and he would certainly be putting an eye in jeopardy. But the farm—he loved the farm. If a fight would make it safe—if a short time of pain and danger would make it free of outside threat—wasn't it worth it? How had he put it himself? "Whatever I have to do to keep the farm, I'll do." What he had to do was take a beating from Girty.

"Will he keep his word?" he asked MacBain.

"Yes," said the smith reluctantly, "I reckon so. But, Harry—"

"I'll do it. Cut him loose."

"Don't be a fool."

"It means the farm."

"Don't be a *fool*. You ain't a match for him. He fights dirty."

"Dirty Girty. Cut him loose."

"No."

"Yes. Don't you see—it's been heading for this all along. Same as the tax quarrel was heading for Concord."

"I won't be no party to it."

Harry stepped forward, bent over Girty, and untied his wrist bindings. "Outside is best, I reckon."

They squared off in front of MacBain's cabin, half bent, arms dangling, swaying, taking each other's measure. Slowly they circled. Girty's hard black eyes glittered, and his big hands clenched, unclenched, clenched, unclenched, eager to get hold of Harry. Until now, their confrontations had always been on Harry's terms, and Harry had always managed to win. Now it would be different.

Girty darted in, caught Harry around the body, and levered him off his feet. Harry went down into the mud, felt his face slide into it. With a quick roll, he got out from under the other and caught Girty's leg. He wasn't strong enough to upend him, but Girty only got away by making a hasty stagger. It gave Harry time to leap up.

Again they circled. Girty pawed him, and Harry ducked. MacBain stood by the doorway, rifle in hand. Girty might beat Harry up, but he wasn't going to escape. The other prisoners had hobbled to the smithy window and were eagerly peering out. From the laundry fire, Maynard watched with enormous eyes.

Girty tried another dart, but this time Harry sidestepped him. He managed to clutch Girty by the hair and get in one solid blow to the throat. (Not good. He'd been aiming for the jaw.) They separated. Then Girty rushed in with his fist raised. Harry's guard came up, but the fist slipped past it, and Harry felt it collide with his face.

The power of the blow was staggering. Harry half-fell,
wits reeling. He was just master enough of himself to
avoid Girty's next rush, but after that it was the most he
could do to get back on his feet. Vision blurred, he spent
the next few minutes dodging. Girty chased him over
most of MacBain's clearing. And yet, even with all that, he
was aware of great satisfaction. He was coming, at last, to
direct grips with his enemy.

It's for the farm, he told himself.

He slipped in the mud, and Girty was on him, pinning
one arm up his back. Pain shot through Harry, and the
more he struggled, the more he hurt. But he managed to

hook one leg around Girty's and apply enough counter pressure that the other's grip was loosened. With tremendous effort, Harry broke free.

Perspiration was running off him now, but Girty seemed scarcely touched. His eyes glittered still, and he was grinning with pleasure. Harry kept his eyes locked, shot a foot out sideways, and successfully tripped Girty. While he sprawled in the mud, Harry flung himself on Girty and for a few seconds kept his face pinned down. Then he was thrown clear.

Again they circled. Harry had a brief impression of Anse moving around the outside like a referee, keeping Girty covered. And perhaps he let his attention wander too far, for suddenly Girty rushed in, got him in that arm-up-the-back position, and while he held him helpless, began to feel for Harry's left eye.

Cold horror came to Harry's aid. It gave him strength he'd never had before, and with one burst he tore out of Girty's grasp and put ten feet between them.

They circled while Harry got his breath back. This was no good. He'd have to have a fight plan, the way he'd had a plan for running his race. Would the same thing work again? Could he turn Girty's own strength against him?

In their movements around the clearing, they had fetched up under a beech that MacBain had decided not to remove. That gave Harry an idea. Trying not to make it look deliberate, he slowly backed up until the fat trunk was immediately behind him. Then he dropped his guard a fraction. Girty could not resist the opening. He rushed in, driving for Harry's face.

At the last possible second, Harry nimbly sidestepped, and the apish frontiersman collided with the tree full force. Clasping both hands to add power, Harry cracked

him across the back of the neck and had the satisfaction of
seeing him go down.

Like lightning, Harry straddled the fallen man and
began to pummel him as hard and as often as he could.
He knew his moment of supremacy wouldn't last long,
and it didn't. Girty tossed him off and staggered to his
feet.

He came up red-eyed and raging and rushed at Harry
with outstretched hands. Harry dodged, ducked, caught
him by a leg and tripped him up, then danced away out of
his reach. Girty rose from his second fall even angrier.

Harry hadn't counted on that, but now he swiftly saw
how to put it to his own advantage. He darted here, there,
teasing Girty, egging him on to rush in, then leaping aside
at the last possible moment. The longer Girty went
without getting his hands on Harry, the oftener he made
his lumbering rushes, the angrier and the clumsier he
became. But Harry had to do something more than
dodge.

The tree business probably wouldn't work again. And if
he tried it, that might set Girty to thinking, and that was
the last thing Harry wanted. But a variation of the tree
business might be effective. There was a great jutting-out
boulder of rock not far off. It dropped off sharply into a
stony little ravine, but if you didn't know the terrain, you
couldn't tell from this side. And Girty didn't know the
terrain.

Gradually Harry backed up, until he could feel stone
underfoot. He let Girty get in a couple of blows, to
encourage him, keep him coming. Now he had to work
him up to clumsy rage again. He feinted a few blows, did
fancy footwork on the stone, and once again pretended to
drop his guard.

Girty rushed. Harry held his stance to the last instant, and then he dropped to a crouch. Girty tripped over him and somersaulted off the rock and into the ravine.

He hit his head on a rock and lay still.

Harry climbed down into the ravine and stood over his enemy, panting. He couldn't believe he had actually done it—defeated Simon Girty on his own terms. He turned the limp body over and searched it. In a pouch attached to his belt, he found the Virginia deed. He removed it and carried it back to the cabin.

MacBain still stood on guard. He goggled when he saw who was returning. "I can't believe it!" he said. "You licked him."

"You might say he licked himself. See, here's the deed."

"By gorries, that's it all right. Let's burn the dad-blamed thing."

"I'm thinking it might be a good idea to hang onto it—or make Girty transfer ownership to Sukey and me."

"You reckon you can do that?"

"Worth a try. If he says no, then we can burn it."

The prisoners were still staring out the cabin window. Their jaws had also dropped at sight of Harry still on his feet and apparently victorious. Anse went inside to see they all remained bound fast, and Harry lingered, wiping off the mud that the fight had left him covered with.

He felt—released. He wondered if those Yankee militiamen felt like this when their Concord battle was over—however it had actually happened. Did they look at one another and say, "Well, we proved it can be done"? Did they feel some kind of climax had been passed? That's how Harry felt.

And he knew suddenly that he should have fought

Girty long ago—faced his enemy and taken his beating if he had to. He'd chosen the frontier. It was up to him to submit to frontier ways, even if it meant scrapping. Backing off from problems was like running away from a threatening dog—he just chases after you, and he can run faster than you can.

Well, Harry had turned and faced his immediate problem. Now what about his long-range one? What about seeing that the Ohio Valley was ruled by Ohio Valley people?

And like a flash he made up his mind. He'd go for a soldier. He'd join that man's militia regiment—or some regiment—and he'd march off to the aid of hated Boston. Because in the long run, that was the only way he could make sure of the farm.

And Harry had no sooner reached a conscious decision than an arm shot across his throat from behind and a hand seized his thigh, and a knee dug into the small of his back.

"I'm agoin' to kill you, greenhorn," Girty growled in his ear. "I'm agoin' to break you in two like a piece of dead wood."

And indeed the agony was so terrible that Harry was certain his spine would snap. He tried to shout, but the sleeve across his windpipe prevented it. He tried to clutch at the shaggy black hair, but his reach was too short. He tried to kick with his free leg, and only succeeded in falling to the ground. There Girty knelt on his back and increased the pressure on neck and back.

I'm going to die, Harry thought wildly, but he could do nothing to stop it. I've saved the farm, but now I'm going to die. . . .

Instead, Girty released Harry with a terrible scream.

Harry rolled over onto his throbbing back, for a moment not caring about anything else. Finally he was able to sit up with a groan and gradually came to awareness of what had happened. Girty was rolling on the ground moaning, clawing at the back of his hunting shirt. And behind him stood—no, drooped—Sukey with a dipper in her hand.

It was a moment longer before Harry understood. She had doused Girty with a ladleful of boiling laundry water.

Weak as she was with lingering illness, she had nonetheless tottered out to save her darling from injury. Now, mission accomplished, she stood shivering in her night rail and bare feet. She swayed, sagging at the knees, flung out her arms in a futile attempt to save herself, and sprawled feebly into the mud. Anse, appearing in the doorway, moved fast but not fast enough.

He tossed the rifle to Harry, then lifted her up, all muddy but triumphant. She said, "He can't do that to Harry."

"No, ma'am," he said. "Will you marry me?"

She drew a long sigh. "Oh," she said wearily, "I suppose I might as well."

18
Freedom Papers

It was the middle of June, and they were standing before the magistrate in Hannastown. Sukey still looked thin and pale from her illness, and yet there was a bridelike glow about her, too. She and MacBain held hands as they exchanged vows, and Harry felt all gooey with sentiment. He was glad his sister had given in to her heart instead of being virtuous.

They had forced Girty to sign over his deed and then had sent him and his men downriver on a raft. It was a triumphal moment when Harry repossessed his own cabin. Then the wait for Sukey to recover her strength for the trip to Pittsburgh and Hannastown. Harry had retained four of the invaders' horses in payment for the ox, so it had been a relatively easy journey.

Harry watched, sheepish and a trifle embarrassed, as MacBain kissed his new wife. "And now, Mrs. MacBain," the smith said grandly, "I got a weddin' present for you. Two, in fact."

"A present?"

"Belle, Maynard—you two don't belong to me no more. I'm agivin' you to my wife."

Sukey's face was a sight to behold—first stupefied, then slowly flushing up all radiant. "Oh, Anse," she managed finally, "I should have trusted you."

Harry wrote up the freedom papers, drawing on his Penn deed for legal-sounding words: "Know all men by these presents . . . witnessed . . . heirs and assigns . . ." Then with the magistrate for witness, Belle and her son were formally freed. Harry was always glad afterwards that his last civilian action had been to help in the freeing of two others, before he went off to seek his own independence.

19
After Word

In the spring of 1778, Simon Girty left Pittsburgh to join the British side in the quarrel and thereafter led Indian raids on the white frontier. He was present, in 1782, at the death by torture of Colonel William Crawford, Washington's friend.

At the request of Congress, the new states of Pennsylvania and Virginia solved their boundary dispute. At a conference between representatives, an agreement was worked out to extend the Mason-Dixon line. It was signed August 31, 1779, and ratified the following year, and the boundary was accordingly surveyed and laid out where it is today.

In 1780 the Pennsylvania Assembly passed a measure providing for gradual emancipation of slavery.